Time and
Time Again

AND OTHER SF

I0665440

Time and Time Again

AND OTHER SF

H. Beam Piper

ÆGYPAN PRESS

Time and Time Again and Other SF
A publication of
Ægypan Press

www.aegypan.com

Table of Contents

The Mercenaries

*D*uncan MacLeod hung up the suit he had taken off, and sealed his shirt, socks and underwear in a laundry envelope bearing his name and identity-number, tossing this into one of the wire baskets provided for the purpose. Then, naked except for the plastic identity disk around his neck, he went over to the desk, turned in his locker key, and passed into the big room beyond.

Four or five young men, probably soldiers on their way to town, were coming through from the other side. Like MacLeod, they wore only the plastic disks they had received in exchange for the metal ones they wore inside the reservation, and they were being searched by attendants who combed through their hair, probed into ears and nostrils, peered into mouths with tiny searchlights, and employed a variety of magnetic and electronic detectors.

To this search MacLeod submitted wearily. He had become quite a connoisseur of security measures in fifteen years' research and development work for a dozen different nations, but the Tonto Basin Research Establishment of the Philadelphia Project exceeded anything he had seen before. There were grey-haired veterans of the old Manhattan Project here, men who had worked with Fermi at Chicago, or with Oppenheimer at Los Alamos, twenty years before, and they swore in amused exasperation when they thought of how the relatively mild regulations of those days had irked them. And yet, the very existence of the Manhattan Project had been kept a secret from all but those engaged in it, and its purpose from most of them. Today, in 1965, there might have been a few wandering tribesmen in Somaliland or the Kirghiz Steppes who had never heard of the Western Union's Philadelphia Project, or of the Fourth Komintern's Red Triumph Five-Year Plan, or of the Islamic Kaliphate's Al-Borak Undertaking, or of the Ibero-American Confederation's Cavor Project, but every literate person in the world knew that the four great power-blocs were racing desperately to hunch the first spaceship to reach the Moon and build the Lunar fortress that would insure world supremacy.

He turned in the nonmagnetic identity disk at the desk on the other side of the search room, receiving the metal one he wore inside the reservation, and with it the key to his inside locker. He put on the clothes he had left behind when he had passed out, and filled his pockets with the miscellany of small articles he had not been allowed to carry off the reservation. He knotted the garish necktie affected by the civilian workers and in particular by members of the MacLeod Research Team to advertise their nonmilitary status, lit his pipe, and walked out into the open gallery beyond.

*K*aren Hilquist was waiting for him there, reclining in one of the metal chairs. She looked cool in the belted white coveralls, with the white turban bound around her yellow hair, and very beautiful, and when he saw her, his heart gave a little bump, like a Geiger responding to an ionizing particle. It always did that, although they had been together for twelve years, and married for ten. Then she saw him and smiled, and he came over, fanning himself with his sun helmet, and dropped into a chair beside her.

"Did you call our center for a jeep?" he asked. When she nodded, he continued: "I thought you would, so I didn't bother."

For a while, they sat silent, looking with bored distaste at the swarm of steel-helmeted Army riflemen and tommy-gunners guarding the transfer platforms and the vehicles gate. A string of trucks had been passed under heavy guard into the clearance compound: they were now unloading supplies onto a platform, at the other side of which other trucks were backed waiting to receive the shipment. A hundred feet of bare concrete and fifty armed soldiers separated these from the men and trucks from the outside, preventing contact.

"And still they can't stop leaks," Karen said softly. "And we get blamed for it."

MacLeod nodded and started to say something, when his attention was drawn by a commotion on the driveway. A big Tucker limousine with an O.D. paint job and the single-starred flag of a brigadier general was approaching, horning impatiently. In the back seat MacLeod could see a heavy-shouldered figure with the face of a bad-tempered great Dane — General Daniel Nayland, the military commander of Tonto Basin. The inside guards jumped to attention and saluted; the barrier shot up as though rocket-propelled, and the car slid through; the barrier slammed down behind it. On the other side, the guards were hurling themselves into a frenzy of saluting. Karen made a face after the receding car and muttered something in Hindustani. She probably didn't know the literal meaning of what she had called General Nayland, but she understood that it was a term of extreme opprobrium.

Her husband contributed: "His idea of Heaven would be a huge research establishment, where he'd be a five-star general, and Galileo, Newton, Priestley, Dalton, Maxwell, Planck and Einstein would be tech sergeants."

"And Marie Curie and Lise Meitner would be Wac corporals," Karen added. "He really hates all of us, doesn't he?"

"He hates our Team," MacLeod replied. "In the first place, we're a lot of civilians, who aren't subject to his regulations and don't have to salute him. We're working under contract with the Western Union, not with the United States Government, and as the United States participates in the Western Union on a treaty basis, our contract has the force of a treaty obligation. It gives us what amounts to extraterritoriality, like Europeans in China during the Nineteenth Century. So we have our own transport, for which he must furnish petrol, and our own armed guard, and we fly our own flag over Team Center, and that gripes him as much as anything else. That and the fact that we're foreigners. So wouldn't he love to make this espionage rap stick on us!"

"And our contract specifically gives the United States the right to take action against us in case we endanger the national security," Karen added. She stuffed her cigarette into the not-too-recently-emptied receiver beside her chair, her blue eyes troubled. "You know, some of us could get shot over this, if we're not careful. Dunc, does it really have to be one of our own people who — ?"

"I don't see how it could be anybody else," MacLeod said. "I don't like the idea anymore than you do, but there it is."

"Well, what are we going to do? Is there nobody whom we can trust?"

"Among the technicians and guards, yes. I could think of a score who are absolutely loyal. But among the Team itself — the top researchers — there's nobody I'd take a chance on but Kato Sugihara."

"Can you even be sure of him? I'd hate to think of him as a traitor, but —"

"I have a couple of reasons for eliminating Kato," MacLeod said. "In the first place, outside nucleonic and binding-force physics, there are only three things he's interested in. Jitterbugging, hand-painted neckties, and Southern-style cooking. If he went over to the Komintern, he wouldn't be able to get any of those. Then, he only spends about half his share of the Team's profits, and turns the rest back into the Team

Fund. He has a credit of about a hundred thousand dollars, which he'd lose by leaving us. And then, there's another thing. Kato's father was killed on Guadalcanal, in 1942, when he was only five. After that he was brought up in the teachings of Bushido by his grandfather, an old-time samurai. Bushido is open to some criticism, but nobody can show where double-crossing your own gang is good Bushido. And today, Japan is allied with the Western Union, and in any case, he wouldn't help the Komintern. The Japs'll forgive Russia for that Mussolini back-stab in 1945 after the Irish start building monuments to Cromwell."

A light-blue jeep, lettered *MacLeod Research Team* in cherry-red, was approaching across the wide concrete apron. MacLeod grinned.

"Here it comes. Fasten your safety belt when you get in; that's Ahmed driving."

Karen looked at her watch. "And it's almost time for dinner. You know, I dread the thought of sitting at the table with the others, and wondering which of them is betraying us."

"Only nine of us, instead of thirteen, and still one is a Judas," MacLeod said. "I suppose there's always a place for Judas, at any table."

*T*he MacLeod Team dined together, apart from their assistants and technicians and students. This was no snobbish attempt at class-distinction: matters of Team policy were often discussed at the big round table, and the more confidential details of their work. People who have only their knowledge and their ideas to sell are wary about bandying either loosely, and the six men and three women who faced each other across the twelve-foot diameter of the teakwood table had no other stock-in-trade.

They were nine people of nine different nationalities, or they were nine people of the common extra-nationality of science. That Duncan MacLeod, their leader, had grown up in the Transvaal and his wife had been born in the Swedish university town of Upsala was typical not only of their own group but of the hundreds of independent research-teams that had sprung up after the Second World War. The scientist-adventurer may have been born of the relentless struggle for scientific armament supremacy among nations and the competition for improved techniques among industrial corporations during the late 1950s and early '60s, but he had been begotten when two masses of uranium came together at the top of a steel tower in New Mexico in 1945. And, because scientific research is pre-eminently a matter of pooling brains and efforts, the independent scientists had banded together into teams whose leaders acquired power greater than that of any *condottiere* captain of Renaissance Italy.

Duncan MacLeod, sitting outwardly relaxed and merry and secretly watchful and bitterly sad, was such a free-captain of science. One by one, the others had rallied around him, not because he was a greater physicist than they, but because he was a bolder, more clever, less scrupulous adventurer, better able to guide them through the maze of international power-politics and the no less ruthless if less nakedly violent world of Big Industry.

There was his wife, Karen Hilquist, the young metallurgist who, before she was twenty-five, had perfected a new hardening process for SKF and an incredibly tough gun-steel for the Bofors works. In the few minutes since they had returned to Team Center, she had managed to change her coveralls for a skirt and blouse, and do something intriguing with her hair.

And there was Kato Sugihara, looking younger than his twenty-eight years, who had begun to demonstrate the existence of whole orders of structure below the level of nuclear particles.

There was Suzanne Maillard, her grey hair upswept from a face that had never been beautiful but which was alive with something rarer than mere beauty: she possessed, at the brink of fifty, a charm and smartness that many women half her age might have envied, and she knew more about cosmic rays than any other person living.

And Adam Lowiewski, his black mustache contrasting so oddly with his silver hair, frantically scribbling equations on his doodling-pad, as though his racing fingers could never keep pace with his brain, and explaining them, with obvious condescension, to the boyish-looking Japanese beside him. He was one of the greatest of living mathematicians by anybody's reckoning — *the* greatest, by his own.

And Sir Neville Lawton, the electronics expert, with thinning red-grey hair and meticulously-clipped mustache, who always gave the impression of being in evening clothes, even when, as now, he was dressed in faded khaki.

And Heym ben-Hillel, the Israeli quantum and wave-mechanics man, his heaping dinner plate an affront to the Laws of Moses, his white hair a fluffy, tangled chaos, laughing at an impassively-delivered joke the English knight had made.

And Rudolf von Heldenfeld, with a thin-lipped killer's mouth and a frozen face that never betrayed its owner's thoughts — he was the specialist in magnetic currents and electromagnetic fields.

And Farida Khouroglu, the Turkish girl whom MacLeod and Karen had found begging in the streets of Istanbul, ten years ago, and who had

grown up following the fortunes of the MacLeod Team on every conti-
nent and in a score of nations. It was doubtful if she had ever had a
day's formal schooling in her life, but now she was secretary of the Team,
with a grasp of physics that would have shamed many a professor. She
had grown up a beauty, too, with the large dark eyes and jet-black hair
and paper-white skin of her race. She and Kato Sugihara were very much
in love.

A good team; the best physics-research team in a power-mad, knowl-
edge-hungry world. MacLeod thought, toying with the stem of his
wineglass, of some of their triumphs: The West Australia Atomic Power
Plant. The Segovia Plutonium Works, which had got them all titled as
Grandees of the restored Spanish Monarchy. The seawater chemical
extraction plant in Puerto Rico, where they had worked for Associated
Enterprises, whose president, Blake Hartley, had later become President
of the United States. The hard-won victory over a seemingly insoluble
problem in the Belgian Congo uranium mines — He thought, too, of
the dangers they had faced together, in a world where soldiers must use
the weapons of science and scientists must learn the arts of violence. Of
the treachery of the Islamic Kaliphate, for whom they had once worked;
of the intrigues and plots which had surrounded them in Spain; of the
many attempted kidnappings and assassinations; of the time in Basra
when they had fought with pistols and tommy guns and snatched-up
clubs and flasks of acid to defend their laboratories.

A good team — before the rot of treason had touched it. He could
almost smell the putrid stench of it, and yet, as he glanced from face to
face, he could not guess the traitor. And he had so little time —

*K*ato Sugihara's voice rose to dominate the murmur of conversation
around the table.

"I think I am getting somewhere on my photon-neutrino-electron
interchange-cycle," he announced. "And I think it can be correlated to
the collapsed-matter research."

"So?" von Heldenfeld looked up in interest. "And not with the
problem of what goes on in the 'hot layer' surrounding the Earth?"

"No, Suzanne talked me out of that idea," the Japanese replied.
"That's just a secondary effect of the effect of cosmic rays and solar
radiations on the order of particles existing at that level. But I think
that I have the key to the problem of collapsing matter to plate the hull
of the spaceship."

"That's interesting," Sir Neville Lawton commented. "How so?"

"Well, you know what happens when a photon comes in contact with the atomic structure of matter," Kato said. "There may be an elastic collision, in which the photon merely bounces off. Macroscopically, that's the effect we call reflection of light. Or there may be an inelastic collision, when the photon hits an atom and knocks out an electron — the old photoelectric effect. Or, the photon may be retained for a while and emitted again relatively unchanged — the effect observed in luminous paint. Or, the photon may penetrate, undergo a change to a neutrino, and either remain in the nucleus of the atom or pass through it, depending upon a number of factors. All this, of course, is old stuff; even the photon-neutrino interchange has been known since the mid-'50s, when the Gamow neutrino-counter was developed. But now we come to what you have been so good as to christen the Sugihara Effect — the neutrino picking up a negative charge and, in effect, turning into an electron, and then losing its charge, turning back into a neutrino, and then, as in the case of metal heated to incandescence, being emitted again as a photon.

"At first, we thought this had no connection with the spaceship insulation problem we are under contract to work out, and we agreed to keep this effect a Team secret until we could find out if it had commercial possibilities. But now, I find that it has a direct connection with the collapsed-matter problem. When the electron loses its negative charge and reverts to a neutrino, there is a definite accretion of interatomic binding-force, and the molecule, or the crystalline lattice or whatever tends to contract, and when the neutrino becomes a photon, the nucleus of the atom contracts."

*H*eym ben-Hillel was sitting oblivious to everything but his young colleague's words, a slice of the flesh of the unclean beast impaled on his fork and halfway to his mouth.

"Yes! Certainly!" he exclaimed. "That would explain so many things I have wondered about: And of course, there are other forces at work which, in the course of nature, balance that effect —"

"But can the process be controlled?" Suzanne Maillard wanted to know. "Can you convert electrons to neutrinos and then to photons in sufficient numbers, and eliminate other effects that would cause compensating atomic and molecular expansion?"

Kato grinned, like a tomcat contemplating the bones of a fish he has just eaten.

"Yes, I can. I have." He turned to MacLeod. "Remember those bullets I got from you?" he asked.

MacLeod nodded. He handloaded for his .38-special, and like all advanced cases of handloading-fever, he was religiously fanatical about uniformity of bullet weights and dimensions. Unlike most handloaders, he had available the instruments to secure such uniformity.

"Those bullets are as nearly alike as different objects can be," Kato said. "They weigh 158 grains, and that means one-five-eight-point-zero-zero-zero-practically-nothing. The diameter is .35903 inches. All right; I've been subjecting those bullets to different radiation-bombardments, and the best results have given me a bullet with a diameter of .35892 inches, and the weight is unchanged. In other words, there's been no loss of mass, but the mass had contracted. And that's only been the first test."

"Well, write up everything you have on it, and we'll lay out further experimental work," MacLeod said. He glanced around the table. "So far, we can't be entirely sure. The shrinkage may be all in the crystalline lattice: the atomic structure may be unchanged. What we need is matter that is really collapsed."

"I'll do that," Kato said. "Barida, I'll have all my data available for you before noon tomorrow: you can make up copies for all Team members."

"Make mine on microfilm, for projection," von Heldenfeld said.

"Mine, too," Sir Neville Lawton added.

"Better make microfilm copies for everybody," Heym ben-Hillel suggested. "They're handier than type-script."

MacLeod rose silently and tiptoed around behind his wife and Rudolf von Heldenfeld, to touch Kato Sugihara on the shoulder.

"Come on outside, Kato," he whispered. "I want to talk to you."

*T*he Japanese nodded and rose, following him outside onto the roof above the laboratories. They walked over to the edge and stopped at the balustrade.

"Kato, when you write up your stuff, I want you to falsify everything you can. Put it in such form that the data will be absolutely worthless, but also in such form that nobody, not even Team members, will know it has been falsified. Can you do that?"

Kato's almond-shaped eyes widened. "Of course I can, Dunc," he replied. "But why — ?"

"I hate to say this, but we have a traitor in the Team. One of those people back in the dining room is selling us out to the Fourth Komintern. I know it's not Karen, and I know it's not you, and that's as much as I do know, now."

The Japanese sucked in his breath in a sharp hiss. "You wouldn't say that unless you were sure, Dunc," he said.

"No. At about 1000 this morning, Dr. Weissberg, the civilian director, called me to his office. I found him very much upset. He told me that General Nayland is accusing us — by which he meant this Team — of furnishing secret information on our subproject to Komintern agents. He said that British Intelligence agents at Smolensk had learned that the Red Triumph laboratories there were working along lines of research originated at MacLeod Team Center here. They relayed the information to Western Union Central Intelligence, and WU passed it on to United States Central Intelligence, and now Counter Espionage is riding Nayland about it, and he's trying to make us the goat."

"He would love to get some of us shot," Kato said. "And that could happen. They took a long time getting tough about espionage in this country, but when Americans get tough about something, they get tough right. But look here; we handed in our progress-reports to Felix Weissberg, and he passed them on to Nayland. Couldn't the leak be right in Nayland's own HQ?"

"That's what I thought, at first," MacLeod replied. "Just wishful thinking, though. Fact is, I went up to Nayland's HQ and had it out with him; accused him of just that. I think I threw enough of a scare into him to hold him for a couple of days. I wanted to know just what it was the Komintern was supposed to have got from us, but he wouldn't tell me. That, of course, was classified-stuff."

"Well?"

"Well then, Karen and I got our digestive tracts emptied and went in to town, where I could use a phone that didn't go through a military switch-board, and I put through a call to Allan Hartley, President Hartley's son. He owes us a break, after the work we did in Puerto Rico. I told him all I wanted was some information to help clear ourselves, and he told me to wait a half an hour and then call Counter Espionage Office in Washington and talk to General Hammond."

"Ha! If Allan Hartley's for us, what are we worried about?" Kato asked. "I always knew he was the power back of Associated Enterprises and his father was the front-man: I'll bet it's the same with the Government."

"Allan Hartley's for us as long as our nose is clean. If we let it get dirty, we get it bloodied, too. We have to clean it ourselves," MacLeod told him. "But here's what Hammond gave me: The Komintern knows all about our collapsed-matter experiments with zinc, titanium and nickel. They know about our theoretical work on cosmic rays, including Suzanne's work up to about a month ago. They know about that effect Sir Neville and Heym discovered two months ago." He paused. "And they know about the photon-neutrino-electron interchange."

Kato responded to this with a gruesome double-take that gave his face the fleeting appearance of an ancient samurai war mask.

"That wasn't included in any report we ever made," he said. "You're right: the leak comes from inside the Team. It must be Sir Neville, or Suzanne, or Heym ben-Hillel, or Adam Lowiewski, or Rudolf von Heldenfeld, or — No! No, I can't believe it could be Farida!" He looked at MacLeod pleadingly. "You don't think she could have — ?"

"No, Kato. The Team's her whole life, even more than it is mine. She came with us when she was only twelve, and grew up with us. She doesn't know any other life than this, and wouldn't want any other. It has to be one of the other five."

"Well, there's Suzanne," Kato began. "She had to clear out of France because of political activities, after the collapse of the Fourth Republic and the establishment of the Rightist Directoire in '57. And she worked with Joliot-Curie, and she was at the University of Louvain in the early '50s, when that place was crawling with Commies."

"And that brings us to Sir Neville," MacLeod added. "He dabbles in spiritualism; he and Suzanne do planchette-séances. A planchette can be manipulated. Maybe Suzanne produced a communication advising Sir Neville to help the Komintern."

"Could be. Then, how about Lowiewski? He's a Pole who can't go back to Poland, and Poland's a Komintern country." Kato pointed out. "Maybe he'd sell us out for amnesty, though why he'd want to go back there, the way things are now — ?"

"His vanity. You know, missionary-school native going back to the village wearing real pants, to show off to the savages. Used to be a standing joke, down where I came from." MacLeod thought for a moment. "And Rudolf: he's always had a poor view of the democratic system of government. He might feel more at home with the Komintern. Of course, the Ruskis killed his parents in 1945 —"

"So what?" Kato retorted. "The Americans killed my father in 1942, but I'm not making an issue out of it. That was another war; Japan's a Western Union country, now. So's Germany — How about Heym, by the way? Remember when the Komintern wanted us to come to Russia and do the same work we're doing here?"

"I remember that after we turned them down, somebody tried to kidnap Karen," MacLeod said grimly. "I remember a couple of Russians got rather suddenly dead trying it, too."

"I wasn't thinking of that. I was thinking of our round-table argument when the proposition was considered. Heym was in favor of accepting. Now that, I would say, indicates either Communist sympathies or an overtrusting nature," Kato submitted. "And a lot of grade-A traitors have been made out of people with trusting natures."

MacLeod got out his pipe and lit it. For a long time, he stared out across the mountain-ringed vista of sagebrush, dotted at wide intervals with the bulks of research-centers and the red roofs of the villages.

"Kato, I think I know how we're going to find out which one it is," he said. "First of all, you write up your data, and falsify it so that it won't do any damage if it gets into Komintern hands. And then —"

*T*he next day started in an atmosphere of suppressed excitement and anxiety, which, beginning with MacLeod and Karen and Kato Sugihara, seemed to communicate itself by contagion to everybody in the MacLeod Team's laboratories. The top researchers and their immediate assistants and students were the first to catch it; they ascribed the tension under which their leader and his wife and the Japanese labored to the recent developments in the collapsed-matter problem. Then, there were about a dozen implicitly-trusted technicians and guards, who had been secretly gathered in MacLeod's office the night before and informed of the crisis that had arisen. Their associates could not miss the fact that they were preoccupied with something unusual.

They were a variegated crew; men who had been added to the Team in every corner of the world. There was Ahmed Abd-el-Rahman, the Arab jeep-driver who had joined them in Basra. There was the wiry little Greek whom everybody called Alex Unpronounceable. There was an Italian, and two Chinese, and a cashiered French Air Force officer, and a Malay, and the son of an English earl who insisted that his name was Bertie Wooster. They had sworn themselves to secrecy, had heard MacLeod's story with a polylingual burst of pious or blasphemous exclamations, and then they had scattered, each to the work assigned him.

MacLeod had risen early and submitted to the ordeal of the search to leave the reservation and go to town again, this time for a conference at the shabby back-street cigar store that concealed a Counter Espionage center. He had returned just as Farida Khouroglu was finishing the microfilm copies of Kato's ingeniously-concocted pseudo-data. These copies were distributed at noon, while the Team was lunching, along with carbons of the original type-script.

He was the first to leave the table, going directly to the basement, where Alex Unpronounceable and the man who had got his alias from the works of P. G. Wodehouse were listening in on the telephone calls going in and out through the Team-center switch-board, and making recordings. For two hours, MacLeod remained with them. He heard Suzanne Maillard and some woman who was talking from a number in the Army married-officers' settlement making arrangements about a party. He heard Rudolf von Heldenfeld make a date with some girl. He listened to a violent altercation between the Team chef and somebody at Army Quartermaster's HQ about the quality of a lot of dressed chicken. He listened to a call that came in for Adam Lowiewski, the mathematician.

"This is Joe," the caller said. "I've got to go to town late this afternoon, but I was wondering if you'd have time to meet me at the Recreation House at Oppenheimer Village for a game of chess. I'm calling from there, now."

"Fine; I can make it," Lowiewski's voice replied. "I'm in the middle of a devil's own mathematical problem; maybe a game of chess would clear my head. I have a new queen's-knight gambit I want to try on you, anyhow."

Bertie Wooster looked up sharply. "Now there; that may be what we're —"

The telephone beside MacLeod rang. He scooped it up; named himself into it.

It was Ahmed Abd-el-Rahman. "Look, chief; I tail this guy to Oppenheimer Village," the Arab, who had learned English from American movies, answered. "He goes into the rec-joint. I slide in after him, an' he ain't in sight. I'm lookin' around for him, see, when he comes bargin' outa the Don Ameche box. Then he grabs a table an' a beer. What next?"

"Stay there; keep an eye on him," MacLeod told him. "If I want you, I'll call."

MacLeod hung up and straightened, feeling under his packet for his .38-special.

"That's it, boys," he said. "Lowiewski. Come on."

"Hah!" Alex Unpronounceable had his gun out and was checking the cylinder. He spoke briefly in description of the Polish mathematician's ancestry, physical characteristics, and probable post-mortem destination. Then he put the gun away, and the three men left the basement.

*F*or minutes that seamed like hours, MacLeod and the Greek waited on the main floor, where they could watch both the elevators and the stairway. Bertie Wooster had gone up to alert Kato Sugihara and Karen. Then the door of one of the elevators opened and Adam Lowiewski emerged, with Kato behind him, apparently lost in a bulky scientific journal he was reading. The Greek moved in from one side, and MacLeod stepped in front of the Pole.

"Hi, Adam," he greeted. "Have you looked into that batch of data yet?"

"Oh, yes. Yes." Lowiewski seemed barely able to keep his impatience within the bounds of politeness. "Of course, it's out of my line, but the mathematics seems sound." He started to move away.

"You're not going anywhere," MacLeod told him. "The chess game is over. The red pawns are taken — the one at Oppenheimer Village, and the one here."

There was a split second in which Lowiewski struggled — almost successfully — to erase the consternation from his face.

"I don't know what you're talking about," he began. His right hand started to slide under his left coat lapel.

MacLeod's Colt was covering him before he could complete the movement. At the same time, Kato Sugihara dropped the paper-bound periodical, revealing the thin-bladed knife he had concealed under it. He stepped forward, pressing the point of the weapon against the Pole's side. With the other hand, he reached across Lowiewski's chest and jerked the pistol from his shoulder-holster. It was one of the elegant little .32 Beretta 1954 Model automatics.

"Into the elevator," MacLeod ordered. An increasing pressure of Kato's knife emphasized the order. "And watch him; don't let him get rid of anything," he added to the Greek.

"If you would explain this outrage —" Lowiewski began. "I assume it is your idea of a joke —"

Without even replying, MacLeod slammed the doors and started the elevator upward, letting it rise six floors to the living quarters. Karen Hilquist and the aristocratic black-sheep who called himself Bertie Wooster were waiting when he opened the door. The Englishman took one of Lowiewski's arms; MacLeod took the other. The rest fell in behind as they hustled the captive down the hall and into the big sound-proofed dining room. They kept Lowiewski standing, well away from any movable object in the room; Alex Unpronounceable took his left arm as MacLeod released it and went to the communicator and punched the all-outlets button.

"Dr. Maillard; Dr. Sir Neville Lawton; Dr. ben-Hillel; Dr. von Held-enfeld; Mlle. Khouroglu," he called. "Dr. MacLeod speaking. Come at once, repeat at once, to the round table — Dr. Maillard; Dr. Sir Neville Lawton —"

*K*aren said something to the Japanese and went outside. For a while, nobody spoke. Kato came over and lit a cigarette in the bowl of MacLeod's pipe. Then the other Team members entered in a body. Evidently Karen had intercepted them in the hallway and warned them that they would find some unusual situation inside; even so, there was a burst of surprised exclamations when they found Adam Lowiewski under detention.

"Ladies and gentlemen," MacLeod said, "I regret to tell you that I have placed our colleague, Dr. Lowiewski, under arrest. He is suspected of betraying confidential data to agents of the Fourth Komintern. Yesterday, I learned that data on all our work here, including Team-secret data on the Sugihara Effect, had got into the hands of the Komintern and was being used in research at the Smolensk laboratories. I also learned that General Nayland blames this Team as a whole with double-dealing and selling this data to the Komintern. I don't need to go into any lengthy exposition of General Nayland's attitude toward this Team, or toward Free Scientists as a class, or toward the research-contract system. Nor do I need to point out that if he pressed these charges against us, some of us could easily suffer death or imprisonment."

"So he had to have a victim in a hurry, and pulled my name out of the hat," Lowiewski sneered.

"I appreciate the gravity of the situation," Sir Neville Lawton said. "And if the Sugihara Effect was among the data betrayed, I can understand that nobody but one of us could have betrayed it. But why, necessarily, should it be Adam? We all have unlimited access to all records and theoretical data."

"Exactly. But collecting information is the smallest and easiest part of espionage. Almost anybody can collect information. Where the spy really earns his pay is in transmitting of information. Now, think of the almost fantastic security measures in force here, and consider how you would get such information, including masses of mathematical data beyond any human power of memorization, out of this reservation."

"Ha, nobody can take anything out," Suzanne Maillard said. "Not even one's breakfast. Is Adam accused of sorcery, too?"

"The only material things that are allowed to leave this reservation are sealed cases of models and data shipped to the different development plants. And the Sugihara Effect never was reported, and wouldn't go out that way," Heym ben-Hillel objected.

"But the data on the Sugihara Effect reached Smolensk," MacLeod replied. "And don't talk about Darwin and Wallace: it wasn't a coincidence. This stuff was taken out of the Tonto Basin Reservation by the only person who could have done so, in the only way that anything could leave the reservation without search. So I had that person shadowed, and at the same time I had our telephone lines tapped, and eavesdropped on all calls entering or leaving this center. And the person who had to be the spy-courier called Adam Lowiewski, and Lowiewski made an appointment to meet him at the Oppenheimer Village Recreation House to play chess."

"Very suspicious, very suspicious," Lowiewski derided. "I receive a call from a friend at the same time that some anonymous suspect is using the phone. There are only five hundred telephone conversations a minute on this reservation."

"Immediately, Dr. Lowiewski attempted to leave this building," MacLeod went on. "When I intercepted him, he tried to draw a pistol. This one." He exhibited the Beretta. "I am now going to have Dr. Lowiewski searched, in the presence of all of you." He nodded to Alex and the Englishman.

*T*hey did their work thoroughly. A pile of Lowiewski's pocket effects was made on the table; as each item was added to it, the Pole made some sarcastic comment.

"And that pack of cigarettes: unopened," he jeered. "I suppose I communicated the data to the manufacturers by telepathy, and they printed it on the cigarette papers in invisible ink."

"Maybe not. Maybe you opened the pack, and then resealed it," Kato suggested. "A heated spatula under the cellophane; like this."

He used the point of his knife to illustrate. The cellophane came unsealed with surprising ease: so did the revenue stamp. He dumped out the contents of the pack: sixteen cigarettes, four cigarette tip-ends, four bits snapped from the other ends — and a small aluminum microfilm capsule.

Lowiewski's face twitched. For an instant, he tried vainly to break loose from the men who held him. Then he slumped into a chair. Heym ben-Hillel gasped in shocked surprise. Suzanne Maillard gave a short, felinelike cry. Sir Neville Lawton looked at the capsule curiously and said: "Well, my sainted Aunt Agatha!"

"That's the capsule I gave him, at noon," Farida Khouroglu exclaimed, picking it up. She opened it and pulled out a roll of colloidex projection film. There was also a bit of cigarette paper in the capsule, upon which a notation had been made in Kyrilic characters.

Rudolf von Heldenfeld could read Russian. "'Data on new development of photon-neutrino-electron interchange. 22 July, '65. Vladmir.' Vladmir, I suppose, is this *schweinhund's* code name," he added.

The film and the paper passed from hand to hand. The other members of the Team sat down; there was a tendency to move away from the chair occupied by Adam Lowiewski. He noticed this and sneered.

"Afraid of contamination from the moral leper?" he asked. "You were glad enough to have me correct your stupid mathematical errors."

Kato Sugihara picked up the capsule, took a final glance at the cigarette pack, and said to MacLeod: "I'll be back as soon as this is done." With that, he left the room, followed by Bertie Wooster and the Greek.

*H*eym ben-Hillel turned to the others: his eyes had the hurt and puzzled look of a dog that has been kicked for no reason. "But why did he do this?" he asked.

"He just told you," MacLeod replied. "He's the great Adam Lowiewski. Checking math for a physics-research team is beneath his dignity. I suppose the Komintern offered him a professorship at Stalin University." He was watching Lowiewski's face keenly. "No," he continued. "It was probably the mathematics chair of the Soviet Academy of Sciences."

"But who was this person who could smuggle microfilm out of the reservation?" Suzanne Maillard wanted to know. "Somebody has invented teleportation, then?"

MacLeod shook his head. "It was General Nayland's chauffeur. It had to be. General Nayland's car is the only thing that gets out of here without being searched. The car itself is serviced at Army vehicles pool; nobody could hide anything in it for a confederate to pick up outside. Nayland is a stuffed shirt of the first stuffing, and a tinpot Hitler to boot, but he is fanatically and incorruptibly patriotic. That leaves the chauffeur. When Nayland's in the car, nobody even sees him; he might as well be a robot steering-device. Old case of Father Brown's Invisible Man. So, since he had to be the courier, all I did was have Ahmed

Abd-el-Rahman shadow him, and at the same time tap our phones. When he contacted Lowiewski, I knew Lowiewski was our traitor."

Sir Neville Lawton gave a strangling laugh. "Oh, my dear Aunt Fanny! And Nayland goes positively crackers on security. He gets goose pimples every time he hears somebody saying '$E = mc^2$' for fear a Komintern spy might hear him. It's a wonder he hasn't put the value of Planck's Constant on the classified list. He sets up all these fantastic search rooms and barriers, and then he drives through the gate, honking his bloody horn, with his chauffeur's pockets full of top secrets. Now I've seen everything!"

"Not quite everything," MacLeod said. "Kato's going to put that capsule in another cigarette pack, and he'll send one of his lab girls to Oppenheimer Village with it, with a message from Lowiewski to the effect that he couldn't get away. And when this chauffeur takes it out, he'll run into a Counter Espionage road-block on the way to town. They'll shoot him, of course, and they'll probably transfer Nayland to the Mississippi Valley Flood Control Project, where he can't do anymore damage. At least, we'll have him out of our hair."

"If we have any hair left," Heym ben-Hillel gloomed. "You've got Nayland into trouble, but you haven't got us out of it."

"What do you mean?" Suzanne Maillard demanded. "He's found the traitor and stopped the leak."

"Yes, but we're still responsible, as a team, for this betrayal," the Israeli pointed out. "This Nayland is only a symptom of the enmity which politicians and militarists feel toward the Free Scientists, and of their opposition to the research-contract system. Now they have a scandal to use. Our part in stopping the leak will be ignored; the publicity will be about the treason of a Free Scientist."

"That's right," Sir Neville Lawton agreed. "And that brings up another point. We simply can't hand this fellow over to the authorities. If we do, we establish a precedent that may wreck the whole system under which we operate."

"Yes: it would be a fine thing if governments start putting Free Scientists on trial and shooting them," Farida Khouroglu supported him. "In a few years, none of us would be safe."

"But," Suzanne cried, "you are not arguing that this species of an animal be allowed to betray us unpunished?"

"Look," Rudolf von Heldenfeld said. "Let us give him his pistol, and one cartridge, and let him remove himself like a gentleman. He will spare himself the humiliation of trial and execution, and us all the embarrassment of having a fellow scientist pilloried as a traitor."

"Now there's a typical Prussian suggestion," Lowiewski said.

Kato Sugihara, returning alone, looked around the table. "Did I miss something interesting?" he asked.

"Oh, very," Lowiewski told him. "Your Junker friend thinks I should perform *seppuku.*"

Kato nodded quickly. "Excellent idea!" he congratulated von Heldenfeld. "If he does, he'll save everybody a lot of trouble. Himself included." He nodded again. "If he does that, we can protect his reputation, after he's dead."

"I don't really see how," Sir Neville objected. "When the Counter Espionage people were brought into this, the thing went out of our control."

"Why, this chauffeur was the spy, as well as the spy-courier," MacLeod said. "The information he transmitted was picked up piecemeal from different indiscreet lab-workers and students attached to our team. Of course, we are investigating, mumble-mumble. Naturally, no one will admit, mumble-mumble. No stone will be left unturned, mumble-mumble. Disciplinary action, mumble-mumble."

"And I suppose he got that microfilm piecemeal, too?" Lowiewski asked.

"Oh, that?" MacLeod shrugged. "That was planted on him. One of our girls arranged an opportunity for him to steal it from her, after we began to suspect him. Of course, Kato falsified everything he put into that report. As information, it's worthless."

"Worthless? It's better than that," Kato grinned. "I'm really sorry the Komintern won't get it. They'd try some of that stuff out with the big betatron at Smolensk, and a microsecond after they'd throw the switch, Smolensk would look worse than Hiroshima did."

"Well, why would our esteemed colleague commit suicide, just at this time?" Karen Hilquist asked.

"Maybe plutonium poisoning." Farida suggested. "He was doing something in the radiation-lab and got some Pu in him, and of course, shooting's not as painful as that. So —"

"Oh, my dear!" Suzanne protested. "That but stinks! The great Adam Lowiewski, descending from his pinnacle of pure mathematics, to perform a vulgar experiment? With actual *things?*" The Frenchwoman gave an exaggerated shudder. "Horrors!"

"Besides, if our people began getting radioactive, somebody would be sure to claim we were endangering the safely of the whole establishment, and the national-security clause would be invoked, and some nosy person would put a Geiger on the dear departed," Sir Neville added.

"Nervous collapse." Karen said. "According to the laity, all scientists are crazy. Crazy people kill themselves. Adam Lowiewski was a scientist. Ergo Adam Lowiewski killed himself. Besides, a nervous collapse isn't instrumentally detectable."

Heym ben-Hillel looked at MacLeod, his eyes troubled.

"But, Dunc; have we the right to put him to death, either by his own hand or by an Army firing squad?" he asked. "Remember he is not only a traitor; he is one of the world's greatest mathematical minds. Have we a right to destroy that mind?"

Von Heldenfeld shouted, banging his fist on the table: "I don't care if he's Gauss and Riemann and Lorenz and Poincare and Minkowski and Whitehead and Einstein, all collapsed into one! The man is a stinking traitor, not only to us, but to all scientists and all sciences! If he doesn't shoot himself, hand him over to the United States, and let them shoot him! Why do we go on arguing?"

*L*owiewski was smiling, now. The panic that had seized him in the hallway below, and the desperation when the cigarette pack had been opened, had left him.

"Now I have a modest proposal, which will solve your difficulties," he said. "I have money, papers, clothing, everything I will need, outside the reservation. Suppose you just let me leave here. Then, if there is any trouble, you can use this fiction about the indiscreet underlings, without the unnecessary embellishment of my suicide —"

Rudolf von Heldenfeld let out an inarticulate roar of fury. For an instant he was beyond words. Then he sprang to his feet.

"Look at him!" he cried. "Look at him, laughing in our faces, for the dupes and fools he thinks we are!" He thrust out his hand toward MacLeod. "Give me the pistol! He won't shoot himself; I'll do it for him!"

"It would work, Dunc. Really, it would," Heym ben-Hillel urged.

"No," Karen Hilquist contradicted. "If he left here, everybody would know what had happened, and we'd be accused of protecting him. If he kills himself, we can get things hushed up: dead traitors are good traitors. But if he remains alive, we must disassociate ourselves from him by handing him over."

"And wreck the prestige of the Team?" Lowiewski asked.

"At least you will not live to see that!" Suzanne retorted.

Heym ben-Hillel put his elbows on the table and his head in his hands. "Is there no solution to this?" he almost wailed.

"Certainly: an obvious solution," MacLeod said, rising. "Rudolf has just stated it. Only I'm leader of this Team, and there are, of course, jobs a team-leader simply doesn't delegate." The safety catch of the Beretta clicked a period to his words.

"No!" The word was wrenched almost physically out of Lowiewski. He, too, was on his feet, a sudden desperate fear in his face. "No! You wouldn't murder me!"

"The term is 'execute,'" MacLeod corrected. Then his arm swung up, and he shot Adam Lowiewski through the forehead.

For an instant, the Pole remained on his feet. Then his knees buckled, and he fell forward against the table, sliding to the floor.

*M*acLeod went around the table, behind Kato Sugihara and Farida Khouroglu and Heym ben-Hillel, and stood looking down at the man he had killed. He dropped the automatic within a few inches of the dead renegade's outstretched hand, then turned to face the others.

"I regret," he addressed them, his voice and face blank of expression, "to announce that our distinguished colleague, Dr. Adam Lowiewski, has committed suicide by shooting, after a nervous collapse resulting from overwork."

Sir Neville Lawton looked critically at the motionless figure on the floor.

"I'm afraid we'll have trouble making that stick, Dunc," he said. "You shot him at about five yards; there isn't a powder mark on him."

"Oh, sorry; I forgot." MacLeod's voice was mockingly contrite. "It was Dr. Lowiewski's expressed wish that his remains be cremated as soon after death as possible, and that funeral services be held over his ashes. The big electric furnace in the metallurgical lab will do, I think."

"But . . . but there'll be all sorts of formalities —" the Englishman protested.

"Now you forget. Our contract," MacLeod reminded him. "We stand upon our contractual immunity: we certainly won't allow any stupid bureaucratic interference with our deceased colleague's wishes. We have a regular M.D. on our payroll, in case anybody has to have a death certificate to keep him happy, but beyond that —" He shrugged.

"It burns me up, though!" Suzanne Maillard cried. "After the space-ship is built, and the Moon is annexed to the Western Union, there will be publicity, and people will eulogize this species of an Iscariot!"

Heym ben-Hillel, who had been staring at MacLeod in shocked unbelief, roused himself.

"Well, why not? Isn't the creator of the Lowiewski function transformations and the rules of inverse probabilities worthy of eulogy?" He turned to MacLeod. "I couldn't have done what you did, but maybe it was for the best. The traitor is dead; the mathematician will live forever."

"You miss the whole point," MacLeod said. "Both of you. It wasn't a question of revenge, like gangsters bumping off a double-crosser. And it wasn't a question of whitewashing Lowiewski for posterity. We are the MacLeod Research Team. We owe no permanent allegiance to, nor acknowledge the authority of, any national sovereignty or any combination of nations. We deal with national governments as with equals. In consequence, we must make and enforce our own laws.

"You must understand that we enjoy this status only on sufferance. The nations of the world tolerate the Free Scientists only because they need us, and because they know they can trust us. Now, no responsible government official is going to be deceived for a moment by this suicide story we've confected. It will be fully understood that Lowiewski was a traitor, and that we found him out and put him to death. And, as a corollary, it will be understood that this Team, as a Team, is fully trustworthy, and that when any individual Team member is found to be untrustworthy, he will be dealt with promptly and without public scandal. In other words, it will be understood, from this time on, that the MacLeod Team is worthy of the status it enjoys and the responsibilities concomitant with it."

He Walked Around the Horses

*T*his tale is based on an authenticated, documented fact. A man vanished –
right out of this world. And where he went –

*In November 1809, an Englishman named Benjamin Bathurst vanished,
inexplicably and utterly.*

*He was en route to Hamburg from Vienna, where he had been serving as his
government's envoy to the court of what Napoleon had left of the Austrian
Empire. At an inn in Perleburg, in Prussia, while examining a change of horses
for his coach, he casually stepped out of sight of his secretary and his valet. He
was not seen to leave the inn yard. He was not seen again, ever.*

At least, not in this continuum. . . .

(From Baron Eugen von Krutz, Minister of Police, to His Excellency
the Count von Berchtenwald, Chancellor to His Majesty Friedrich
Wilhelm III of Prussia.)

25 November, 1809

Your Excellency:

A circumstance has come to the notice of this Ministry, the signifi-
cance of which I am at a loss to define, but, since it appears to involve
matters of State, both here and abroad, I am convinced that it is of
sufficient importance to be brought to your personal attention. Frankly,
I am unwilling to take any further action in the matter without your
advice.

Briefly, the situation is this: We are holding, here at the Ministry of
Police, a person giving his name as Benjamin Bathurst, who claims to
be a British diplomat. This person was taken into custody by the police
at Perleburg yesterday, as a result of a disturbance at an inn there; he is
being detained on technical charges of causing disorder in a public place,
and of being a suspicious person. When arrested, he had in his possession a dispatch case, containing a number of papers; these are of such

an extraordinary nature that the local authorities declined to assume any responsibility beyond having the man sent here to Berlin.

After interviewing this person and examining his papers, I am, I must confess, in much the same position. This is not, I am convinced, any ordinary police matter; there is something very strange and disturbing here. The man's statements, taken alone, are so incredible as to justify the assumption that he is mad. I cannot, however, adopt this theory, in view of his demeanor, which is that of a man of perfect rationality, and because of the existence of these papers. The whole thing is mad; incomprehensible!

The papers in question accompany, along with copies of the various statements taken at Perleburg, a personal letter to me from my nephew, Lieutenant Rudolf von Tarlburg. This last is deserving of your particular attention; Lieutenant von Tarlburg is a very level-headed young officer, not at all inclined to be fanciful or imaginative. It would take a good deal to affect him as he describes.

The man calling himself Benjamin Bathurst is now lodged in an apartment here at the Ministry; he is being treated with every consideration, and, except for freedom of movement, accorded every privilege.

I am, most anxiously awaiting your advice, et cetera, et cetera,

Krutz

(Report of Traugott Zeller, *Oberwachtmeister, Staatspolizei*, made at Perleburg, 25 November, 1809.)

At about ten minutes past two of the afternoon of Saturday, 25 November, while I was at the police station, there entered a man known to me as Franz Bauer, an inn servant employed by Christian Hauck, at the sign of the Sword & Scepter, here in Perleburg. This man Franz Bauer made complaint to *Staatspolizeikapitan* Ernst Hartenstein, saying that there was a madman making trouble at the inn where he, Franz Bauer, worked. I was, therefore, directed, by *Staatspolizeikapitan* Hartenstein, to go to the Sword & Scepter Inn, there to act at discretion to maintain the peace.

Arriving at the inn in company with the said Franz Bauer, I found a considerable crowd of people in the common room, and, in the midst of them, the innkeeper, Christian Hauck, in altercation with a stranger. This stranger was a gentlemanly-appearing person, dressed in traveling clothes, who had under his arm a small leather dispatch case. As I entered, I could hear him, speaking in German with a strong English accent, abusing the innkeeper, the said Christian Hauck, and accusing him of having drugged his, the stranger's, wine, and of having stolen his, the stranger's, coach-and-four, and of having abducted his, the stranger's, secretary and servants. This the said Christian Hauck was loudly denying, and the other people in the inn were taking the innkeeper's part, and mocking the stranger for a madman.

On entering, I commanded everyone to be silent, in the king's name, and then, as he appeared to be the complaining party of the dispute, I required the foreign gentleman to state to me what was the trouble. He then repeated his accusations against the innkeeper, Hauck, saying that Hauck, or, rather, another man who resembled Hauck and who had claimed to be the innkeeper, had drugged his wine and stolen his coach and made off with his secretary and his servants. At this point, the innkeeper and the bystanders all began shouting denials and contradictions, so that I had to pound on a table with my truncheon to command silence.

I then required the innkeeper, Christian Hauck, to answer the charges which the stranger had made; this he did with a complete denial of all of them, saying that the stranger had had no wine in his inn, and that he had not been inside the inn until a few minutes before, when he had burst in shouting accusations, and that there had been no secretary, and no valet, and no coachman, and no coach-and-four, at the inn, and that the gentleman was raving mad. To all this, he called the people who were in the common room to witness.

I then required the stranger to account for himself. He said that his name was Benjamin Bathurst, and that he was a British diplomat, returning to England from Vienna. To prove this, he produced from his dispatch case sundry papers. One of these was a letter of safe-conduct, issued by the Prussian Chancellery, in which he was named and described as Benjamin Bathurst. The other papers were English, all bearing seals, and appearing to be official documents.

Accordingly, I requested him to accompany me to the police station, and also the innkeeper, and three men whom the innkeeper wanted to bring as witnesses.

Traugott Zeller
Oberwachtmeister

Report approved,

Ernst Hartenstein
Staatspolizeikapitan

(Statement of the self-so-called Benjamin Bathurst, taken at the police station at Perleburg, 25 November, 1809.)

My name is Benjamin Bathurst, and I am Envoy Extraordinary and Minister Plenipotentiary of the government of His Britannic Majesty to the court of His Majesty Franz I, Emperor of Austria, or, at least, I was until the events following the Austrian surrender made necessary my return to London. I left Vienna on the morning of Monday, the 20th, to go to Hamburg to take ship home; I was traveling in my own coach-and-four, with my secretary, Mr. Bertram Jardine, and my valet, William Small, both British subjects, and a coachman, Josef Bidek, an Austrian subject, whom I had hired for the trip. Because of the presence of French troops, whom I was anxious to avoid, I was forced to make a detour west as far as Salzburg before turning north toward Magdeburg, where I crossed the Elbe. I was unable to get a change of horses for my coach after leaving Gera, until I reached Perleburg, where I stopped at the Sword & Scepter Inn.

Arriving there, I left my coach in the inn yard, and I and my secretary, Mr. Jardine, went into the inn. A man, not this fellow here, but another rogue, with more beard and less paunch, and more shabbily dressed, but as like him as though he were his brother, represented himself as the innkeeper, and I dealt with him for a change of horses, and ordered a bottle of wine for myself and my secretary, and also a pot of beer apiece for my valet and the coachman, to be taken outside to them. Then Jardine and I sat down to our wine, at a table in the common room, until the man who claimed to be the innkeeper came back and told us that the fresh horses were harnessed to the coach and ready to go. Then we went outside again.

I looked at the two horses on the off side, and then walked around in front of the team to look at the two nigh-side horses, and as I did I felt giddy, as though I were about to fall, and everything went black before my eyes. I thought I was having a fainting spell, something I am not at all subject to, and I put out my hand to grasp the hitching bar, but could not find it. I am sure, now, that I was unconscious for some time, because when my head cleared, the coach and horses were gone, and in their place was a big farm wagon, jacked up in front, with the right front wheel off, and two peasants were greasing the detached wheel.

I looked at them for a moment, unable to credit my eyes, and then I spoke to them in German, saying, "Where the devil's my coach-and-four?"

They both straightened, startled: the one who was holding the wheel almost dropped it.

"Pardon, excellency," he said, "there's been no coach-and-four here, all the time we've been here."

"Yes," said his mate, "and we've been here since just after noon."

I did not attempt to argue with them. It occurred to me — and it is still my opinion — that I was the victim of some plot; that my wine had been drugged, that I had been unconscious for some time, during which my coach had been removed and this wagon substituted for it, and that these peasants had been put to work on it and instructed what to say if questioned. If my arrival at the inn had been anticipated, and everything put in readiness, the whole business would not have taken ten minutes.

I therefore entered the inn, determined to have it out with this rascally innkeeper, but when I returned to the common room, he was nowhere to be seen, and this other fellow, who has given his name as Christian Hauck, claimed to be the innkeeper and denied knowledge of any of the things I have just stated. Furthermore, there were four cavalrymen, Uhlans, drinking beer and playing cards at the table where Jardine and I had had our wine, and they claimed to have been there for several hours.

I have no idea why such an elaborate prank, involving the participation of many people, should be played on me, except at the instigation of the French. In that case, I cannot understand why Prussian soldiers should lend themselves to it.

Benjamin Bathurst

(Statement of Christian Hauck, innkeeper, taken at the police station at Perleburg, 25 November, 1809.)

May it please your honor, my name is Christian Hauck, and I keep an inn at the sign of the Sword & Scepter, and have these past fifteen years, and my father, and his father, before me, for the past fifty years, and never has there been a complaint like this against my inn. Your honor, it is a hard thing for a man who keeps a decent house, and pays his taxes, and obeys the laws, to be accused of crimes of this sort.

I know nothing of this gentleman, nor of his coach, nor his secretary, nor his servants; I never set eyes on him before he came bursting into the inn from the yard, shouting and raving like a madman, and crying out, "Where the devil's that rogue of an innkeeper?"

I said to him, "I am the innkeeper; what cause have you to call me a rogue, sir?"

The stranger replied:

"You're not the innkeeper I did business with a few minutes ago, and he's the rascal I want to see. I want to know what the devil's been done with my coach, and what's happened to my secretary and my servants."

I tried to tell him that I knew nothing of what he was talking about, but he would not listen, and gave me the lie, saying that he had been drugged and robbed, and his people kidnapped. He even had the impudence to claim that he and his secretary had been sitting at a table in that room, drinking wine, not fifteen minutes before, when there had been four noncommissioned officers of the Third Uhlans at that table since noon. Everybody in the room spoke up for me, but he would not listen, and was shouting that we were all robbers, and kidnapers, and French spies, and I don't know what all, when the police came.

Your honor, the man is mad. What I have told you about this is the truth, and all that I know about this business, so help me God.

Christian Hauck

(Statement of Franz Bauer, inn servant, taken at the police station at Perleburg, 25 November, 1809.)

May it please your honor, my name is Franz Bauer, and I am a servant at the Sword & Scepter Inn, kept by Christian Hauck.

This afternoon, when I went into the inn yard to empty a bucket of slops on the dung heap by the stables, I heard voices and turned around, to see this gentleman speaking to Wilhelm Beick and Fritz Herzer, who were greasing their wagon in the yard. He had not been in the yard when I had turned away to empty the bucket, and I thought that he must have come in from the street. This gentleman was asking Beick and Herzer where was his coach, and when they told him they didn't know, he turned and ran into the inn.

Of my own knowledge, the man had not been inside the inn before then, nor had there been any coach, or any of the people he spoke of, at the inn, and none of the things he spoke of happened there, for otherwise I would know, since I was at the inn all day.

When I went back inside, I found him in the common room shouting at my master, and claiming that he had been drugged and robbed. I saw that he was mad and was afraid that he would do some mischief, so I went for the police.

Franz Bauer
his (x) mark

(Statements of Wilhelm Beick and Fritz Herzer, peasants, taken at the police station at Perleburg, 25 November, 1809.)

May it please your honor, my name is Wilhelm Beick, and I am a tenant on the estate of the Baron von Hentig. On this day, I and Fritz Herzer were sent into Perleburg with a load of potatoes and cabbages which the innkeeper at the Sword & Scepter had bought from the estate superintendent. After we had unloaded them, we decided to grease our wagon, which was very dry, before going back, so we unhitched and began working on it. We took about two hours, starting just after we had eaten lunch, and in all that time, there was no coach-and-four in the inn yard. We were just finishing when this gentleman spoke to us, demanding to know where his coach was. We told him that there had been no coach in the yard all the time we had been there, so he turned around and ran into the inn. At the time, I thought that he had come out of the inn before speaking to us, for I know that he could not have come in from the street. Now I do not know where he came from, but I know that I never saw him before that moment.

Wilhelm Beick
his (x) mark

I have heard the above testimony, and it is true to my own knowledge, and I have nothing to add to it.

Fritz Herzer
his (x) mark

(From *Staatspolizeikapitan* Ernst Hartenstein, to His Excellency, the Baron von Krutz, Minister of Police.)

25 November, 1809

Your Excellency:

The accompanying copies of statements taken this day will explain how the prisoner, the self-so-called Benjamin Bathurst, came into my custody. I have charged him with causing disorder and being a suspicious person, to hold him until more can be learned about him. However, as he represents himself to be a British diplomat, I am unwilling to assume any further responsibility, and am having him sent to your excellency, in Berlin.

In the first place, your excellency, I have the strongest doubts of the man's story. The statement which he made before me, and signed, is bad enough, with a coach-and-four turning into a farm wagon, like Cinderella's coach into a pumpkin, and three people vanishing as though swallowed by the earth. But all this is perfectly reasonable and credible, beside the things he said to me, of which no record was made.

Your excellency will have noticed, in his statement, certain allusions to the Austrian surrender, and to French troops in Austria. After his statement had been taken down, I noticed these allusions, and I inquired, what surrender, and what were French troops doing in Austria. The man looked at me in a pitying manner, and said:

"News seems to travel slowly, hereabouts; peace was concluded at Vienna on the 14th of last month. And as for what French troops are doing in Austria, they're doing the same things Bonaparte's brigands are doing everywhere in Europe."

"And who is Bonaparte?" I asked.

He stared at me as though I had asked him, "Who is the Lord Jehovah?" Then, after a moment, a look of comprehension came into his face.

"So, you Prussians concede him the title of Emperor, and refer to him as Napoleon," he said. "Well, I can assure you that His Britannic Majesty's government haven't done so, and never will; not so long as one Englishman has a finger left to pull a trigger. General Bonaparte is a usurper; His Britannic Majesty's government do not recognize any sovereignty in France except the House of Bourbon." This he said very sternly, as though rebuking me.

It took me a moment or so to digest that, and to appreciate all its implications. Why, this fellow evidently believed, as a matter of fact, that the French Monarchy had been overthrown by some military adventurer named Bonaparte, who was calling himself the Emperor Napoleon, and who had made war on Austria and forced a surrender. I made no attempt to argue with him — one wastes time arguing with madmen — but if this man could believe that, the transformation of a coach-and-four into a cabbage wagon was a small matter indeed. So, to humor him, I asked him if he thought General Bonaparte's agents were responsible for his trouble at the inn.

"Certainly," he replied. "The chances are they didn't know me to see me, and took Jardine for the minister, and me for the secretary, so they made off with poor Jardine. I wonder, though, that they left me my dispatch case. And that reminds me; I'll want that back. Diplomatic papers, you know."

I told him, very seriously, that we would have to check his credentials. I promised him I would make every effort to locate his secretary and his servants and his coach, took a complete description of all of them, and persuaded him to go into an upstairs room, where I kept him under guard. I did start inquiries, calling in all my informers and spies, but, as I expected, I could learn nothing. I could not find anybody, even, who had seen him anywhere in Perleburg before he appeared at the Sword & Scepter, and that rather surprised me, as somebody should have seen him enter the town, or walk along the street.

In this connection, let me remind your excellency of the discrepancy in the statements of the servant, Franz Bauer, and of the two peasants. The former is certain the man entered the inn yard from the street; the latter are just as positive that he did not. Your excellency, I do not like such puzzles, for I am sure that all three were telling the truth to the best of their knowledge. They are ignorant common folk, I admit, but they should know what they did or did not see.

After I got the prisoner into safekeeping, I fell to examining his papers, and I can assure your excellency that they gave me a shock. I had paid little heed to his ravings about the King of France being dethroned, or about this General Bonaparte who called himself the Emperor Napoleon, but I found all these things mentioned in his papers and dispatches, which had every appearance of being official documents. There was repeated mention of the taking, by the French, of Vienna, last May, and of the capitulation of the Austrian Emperor to this General Bonaparte, and of battles being fought all over Europe, and I don't know what other fantastic things. Your excellency, I have heard of all sorts of madmen — one believing himself to be the Archangel Gabriel, or Mohammed, or a werewolf, and another convinced that his bones are made of glass, or that he is pursued and tormented by devils — but so help me God, this is the first time I have heard of a madman who had documentary proof for his delusions! Does your excellency wonder, then, that I want no part of this business?

But the matter of his credentials was even worse. He had papers, sealed with the seal of the British Foreign Office, and to every appearance genuine — but they were signed, as Foreign Minister, by one George Canning, and all the world knows that Lord Castlereagh has been Foreign Minister these last five years. And to cap it all, he had a safe-conduct, sealed with the seal of the Prussian Chancellery — the very seal, for I compared it, under a strong magnifying glass, with one that I knew to be genuine, and they were identical! — and yet, this letter was signed, as Chancellor, not by Count von Berchtenwald, but by Baron Stein, the Minister of Agriculture, and the signature, as far as I could see, appeared to be genuine! This is too much for me, your excellency; I must ask to be excused from dealing with this matter, before I become as mad as my prisoner!

I made arrangements, accordingly, with Colonel Keitel, of the Third Uhlans, to furnish an officer to escort this man into Berlin. The coach in which they come belongs to this police station, and the driver is one of my men. He should be furnished expense money to get back to Perleburg. The guard is a corporal of Uhlans, the orderly of the officer.

He will stay with the *Herr Oberleutnant,* and both of them will return here at their own convenience and expense.

I have the honor, your excellency, to be, et cetera, et cetera.

Ernst Hartenstein
Staatspolizeikapitan

(From *Oberleutnant* Rudolf von Tarlburg, to Baron Eugen von Krutz.)

26 November, 1809

Dear Uncle Eugen;

This is in no sense a formal report; I made that at the Ministry, when I turned the Englishman and his papers over to one of your officers — a fellow with red hair and a face like a bulldog. But there are a few things which you should be told, which wouldn't look well in an official report, to let you know just what sort of a rare fish has got into your net.

I had just come in from drilling my platoon, yesterday, when Colonel Keitel's orderly told me that the colonel wanted to see me in his quarters. I found the old fellow in undress in his sitting room, smoking his big pipe.

"Come in, lieutenant; come in and sit down, my boy!" he greeted me, in that bluff, hearty manner which he always adopts with his junior officers when he has some particularly nasty job to be done. "How would you like to take a little trip in to Berlin? I have an errand, which won't take half an hour, and you can stay as long as you like, just so you're back by Thursday, when your turn comes up for road patrol."

Well, I thought, this is the bait. I waited to see what the hook would look like, saying that it was entirely agreeable with me, and asking what his errand was.

"Well, it isn't for myself, Tarlburg," he said. "It's for this fellow Hartenstein, the *Staatspolizeikapitan* here. He has something he wants done at the Ministry of Police, and I thought of you because I've heard you're related to the Baron von Krutz. You are, aren't you?" he asked, just as though he didn't know all about who all his officers are related to.

"That's right, colonel; the baron is my uncle," I said. "What does Hartenstein want done?"

"Why, he has a prisoner whom he wants taken to Berlin and turned over at the Ministry. All you have to do is to take him in, in a coach, and see he doesn't escape on the way, and get a receipt for him, and for some papers. This is a very important prisoner; I don't think Hartenstein has anybody he can trust to handle him. The prisoner claims to be some sort of a British diplomat, and for all Hartenstein knows, maybe he is. Also, he is a madman."

"A madman?" I echoed.

"Yes, just so. At least, that's what Hartenstein told me. I wanted to know what sort of a madman — there are various kinds of madmen, all of whom must be handled differently — but all Hartenstein would tell me was that he had unrealistic beliefs about the state of affairs in Europe."

"Ha! What diplomat hasn't?" I asked.

Old Keitel gave a laugh, somewhere between the bark of a dog and the croaking of a raven.

"Yes, exactly! The unrealistic beliefs of diplomats are what soldiers die of," he said. "I said as much to Hartenstein, but he wouldn't tell me anything more. He seemed to regret having said even that much. He looked like a man who's seen a particularly terrifying ghost." The old man puffed hard at his famous pipe for a while, blowing smoke through his mustache. "Rudi, Hartenstein has pulled a hot potato out of the ashes, this time, and he wants to toss it to your uncle, before he burns his fingers. I think that's one reason why he got me to furnish an escort for his Englishman. Now, look; you must take this unrealistic diplomat, or this undiplomatic madman, or whatever in blazes he is, in to Berlin. And understand this." He pointed his pipe at me as though it were a pistol. "Your orders are to take him there and turn him over at the Ministry of Police. Nothing has been said about whether you turn him over alive, or dead, or half one and half the other. I know nothing about this business, and want to know nothing; if Hartenstein wants us to play goal warders for him, then he must be satisfied with our way of doing it!"

Well, to cut short the story, I looked at the coach Hartenstein had placed at my disposal, and I decided to chain the left door shut on the outside, so that it couldn't be opened from within. Then, I would put my prisoner on my left, so that the only way out would be past me. I decided not to carry any weapons which he might be able to snatch from me, so I took off my saber and locked it in the seat box, along with the dispatch case containing the Englishman's papers. It was cold enough to wear a greatcoat in comfort, so I wore mine, and in the right side pocket, where my prisoner couldn't reach, I put a little leaded bludgeon, and also a brace of pocket pistols. Hartenstein was going to furnish me a guard as well as a driver, but I said that I would take a servant, who could act as guard. The servant, of course, was my orderly, old Johann; I gave him my double hunting gun to carry, with a big charge of boar shot in one barrel and an ounce ball in the other.

In addition, I armed myself with a big bottle of cognac. I thought that if I could shoot my prisoner often enough with that, he would give me no trouble.

As it happened, he didn't, and none of my precautions — except the cognac — were needed. The man didn't look like a lunatic to me. He was a rather stout gentleman, of past middle age, with a ruddy complexion and an intelligent face. The only unusual thing about him was his hat, which was a peculiar contraption, looking like a pot. I put him in the carriage, and then offered him a drink out of my bottle, taking one about half as big myself. He smacked his lips over it and said, "Well, that's real brandy; whatever we think of their detestable politics, we can't criticize the French for their liquor." Then, he said, "I'm glad they're sending me in the custody of a military gentleman, instead of a confounded gendarme. Tell me the truth, lieutenant; am I under arrest for anything?"

"Why," I said, "Captain Hartenstein should have told you about that. All I know is that I have orders to take you to the Ministry of Police, in Berlin, and not to let you escape on the way. These orders I will carry out; I hope you don't hold that against me."

He assured me that he did not, and we had another drink on it — I made sure, again, that he got twice as much as I did — and then the coachman cracked his whip and we were off for Berlin.

Now, I thought, I am going to see just what sort of a madman this is, and why Hartenstein is making a State affair out of a squabble at an inn. So I decided to explore his unrealistic beliefs about the state of affairs in Europe.

After guiding the conversation to where I wanted it, I asked him:

"What, *Herr* Bathurst, in your belief, is the real, underlying cause of the present tragic situation in Europe?"

That, I thought, was safe enough. Name me one year, since the days of Julius Caesar, when the situation in Europe hasn't been tragic! And it worked, to perfection.

"In my belief," says this Englishman, "the whole mess is the result of the victory of the rebellious colonists in North America, and their blasted republic."

Well, you can imagine, that gave me a start. All the world knows that the American Patriots lost their war for independence from England; that their army was shattered, that their leaders were either killed or driven into exile. How many times, when I was a little boy, did I not sit up long past my bedtime, when old Baron von Steuben was a guest at Tarlburg-Schloss, listening open-mouthed and wide-eyed to his stories of that gallant lost struggle! How I used to shiver at his tales of the terrible winter camp, or thrill at the battles, or weep as he told how he held the dying Washington in his arms, and listened to his noble last words, at the Battle of Doylestown! And here, this man was telling me that the Patriots had really won, and set up the republic for which they had fought! I had been prepared for some of what Hartenstein had called unrealistic beliefs, but nothing as fantastic as this.

"I can cut it even finer than that," Bathurst continued. "It was the defeat of Burgoyne at Saratoga. We made a good bargain when we got Benedict Arnold to turn his coat, but we didn't do it soon enough. If he hadn't been on the field that day, Burgoyne would have gone through Gates' army like a hot knife through butter."

But Arnold hadn't been at Saratoga. I know; I have read much of the American War. Arnold was shot dead on New Year's Day of 1776, during the storming of Quebec. And Burgoyne had done just as Bathurst had said; he had gone through Gates like a knife, and down the Hudson to join Howe.

"But, *Herr* Bathurst," I asked, "how could that affect the situation in Europe? America is thousands of miles away, across the ocean."

"Ideas can cross oceans quicker than armies. When Louis XVI decided to come to the aid of the Americans, he doomed himself and his regime. A successful resistance to royal authority in America was all the French Republicans needed to inspire them. Of course, we have Louis's own weakness to blame, too. If he'd given those rascals a whiff of grapeshot, when the mob tried to storm Versailles in 1790, there'd have been no French Revolution."

But he had. When Louis XVI ordered the howitzers turned on the mob at Versailles, and then sent the dragoons to ride down the survivors, the Republican movement had been broken. That had been when Cardinal Talleyrand, who was then merely Bishop of Autun, had came to the fore and become the power that he is today in France; the greatest King's Minister since Richelieu.

"And, after that, Louis's death followed as surely as night after day," Bathurst was saying. "And because the French had no experience in self-government, their republic was foredoomed. If Bonaparte hadn't seized power, somebody else would have; when the French murdered their king, they delivered themselves to dictatorship. And a dictator, unsupported by the prestige of royalty, has no choice but to lead his people into foreign war, to keep them from turning upon him."

It was like that all the way to Berlin. All these things seem foolish, by daylight, but as I sat in the darkness of that swaying coach, I was almost convinced of the reality of what he told me. I tell you, Uncle Eugen, it was frightening, as though he were giving me a view of Hell.

Gott im Himmel, the things that man talked of! Armies swarming over Europe; sack and massacre, and cities burning; blockades, and starvation; kings deposed, and thrones tumbling like tenpins; battles in which the soldiers of every nation fought, and in which tens of thousands were mowed down like ripe grain; and, over all, the Satanic figure of a little man in a grey coat, who dictated peace to the Austrian Emperor in Schoenbrunn, and carried the Pope away a prisoner to Savona.

Madman, eh? Unrealistic beliefs, says Hartenstein? Well, give me madmen who drool spittle, and foam at the mouth, and shriek obscene blasphemies. But not this pleasant-seeming gentleman who sat beside me and talked of horrors in a quiet, cultured voice, while he drank my cognac.

But not all my cognac! If your man at the Ministry — the one with red hair and the bulldog face — tells you that I was drunk when I brought in that Englishman, you had better believe him!

Rudi

(From Count von Berchtenwald, to the British Minister.)

28 November, 1809

Honored Sir:

The accompanying dossier will acquaint you with the problem confronting this Chancellery, without needless repetition on my part. Please to understand that it is not, and never was, any part of the intentions of the government of His Majesty Friedrich Wilhelm III to offer any injury or indignity to the government of His Britannic Majesty George III. We would never contemplate holding in arrest the person, or tampering with the papers, of an accredited envoy of your government. However, we have the gravest doubt, to make a considerable understatement, that this person who calls himself Benjamin Bathurst is any such envoy, and we do not think that it would be any service to the government of His Britannic Majesty to allow an impostor to travel about Europe in the guise of a British diplomatic representative. We certainly should not thank the government of His Britannic Majesty for failing to take steps to deal with some person who, in England, might falsely represent himself to be a Prussian diplomat.

This affair touches us as closely as it does your own government; this man had in his possession a letter of safe-conduct, which you will find in the accompanying dispatch case. It is of the regular form, as issued by this Chancellery, and is sealed with the Chancellery seal, or with a very exact counterfeit of it. However, it has been signed, as Chancellor

of Prussia, with a signature indistinguishable from that of the Baron
Stein, who is the present Prussian Minister of Agriculture. Baron Stein
was shown the signature, with the rest of the letter covered, and without
hesitation acknowledged it for his own writing. However, when the letter
was uncovered and shown to him, his surprise and horror were such as
would require the pen of a Goethe or a Schiller to describe, and he
denied categorically ever having seen the document before.

I have no choice but to believe him. It is impossible to think that a
man of Baron Stein's honorable and serious character would be party
to the fabrication of a paper of this sort. Even aside from this, I am in
the thing as deeply as he; if it is signed with his signature, it is also sealed
with my seal, which has not been out of my personal keeping in the ten
years that I have been Chancellor here. In fact, the word "impossible"
can be used to describe the entire business. It was impossible for the
man Benjamin Bathurst to have entered the inn yard — yet he did. It
was impossible that he should carry papers of the sort found in his
dispatch case, or that such papers should exist — yet I am sending them
to you with this letter. It is impossible that Baron von Stein should sign
a paper of the sort he did, or that it should be sealed by the Chancellery
— yet it bears both Stein's signature and my seal.

You will also find in the dispatch case other credentials, ostensibly
originating with the British Foreign Office, of the same character, being
signed by persons having no connection with the Foreign Office, or
even with the government, but being sealed with apparently authentic
seals. If you send these papers to London, I fancy you will find that they
will there create the same situation as that caused here by this letter of
safe-conduct.

I am also sending you a charcoal sketch of the person who calls
himself Benjamin Bathurst. This portrait was taken without its subject's
knowledge. Baron von Krutz's nephew, Lieutenant von Tarlburg, who
is the son of our mutual friend Count von Tarlburg, has a little friend,
a very clever young lady who is, as you will see, an expert at this sort of
work: she was introduced into a room at the Ministry of Police and
placed behind a screen, where she could sketch our prisoner's face. If
you should send this picture to London, I think that there is a good
chance that it might be recognized. I can vouch that it is an excellent
likeness.

To tell the truth, we are at our wits' end about this affair. I cannot
understand how such excellent imitations of these various seals could
be made, and the signature of the Baron von Stein is the most expert
forgery that I have ever seen, in thirty years' experience as a statesman.
This would indicate careful and painstaking work on the part of some-

body; how, then, do we reconcile this with such clumsy mistakes, recognizable as such by any schoolboy, as signing the name of Baron Stein as Prussian Chancellor, or Mr. George Canning, who is a member of the opposition party and not connected with your government, as British Foreign secretary.

These are mistakes which only a madman would make. There are those who think our prisoner is mad, because of his apparent delusions about the great conqueror, General Bonaparte, alias the Emperor Napoleon. Madmen have been known to fabricate evidence to support their delusions, it is true, but I shudder to think of a madman having at his disposal the resources to manufacture the papers you will find in this dispatch case. Moreover, some of our foremost medical men, who have specialized in the disorders of the mind, have interviewed this man Bathurst and say that, save for his fixed belief in a nonexistent situation, he is perfectly sane.

Personally, I believe that the whole thing is a gigantic hoax, perpetrated for some hidden and sinister purpose, possibly to create confusion, and to undermine the confidence existing between your government and mine, and to set against one another various persons connected with both governments, or else as a mask for some other conspiratorial activity. Only a few months ago, you will recall, there was a Jacobin plot unmasked at Köln.

But, whatever this business may portend, I do not like it. I want to get to the bottom of it as soon as possible, and I will thank you, my dear sir, and your government, for any assistance you may find possible.

I have the honor, sir, to be, et cetera, et cetera, et cetera,

Berchtenwald

FROM BARON VON KRUTZ, TO THE COUNT VON BERCHTENWALD. MOST URGENT; MOST IMPORTANT. TO BE DELIVERED IMMEDIATELY AND IN PERSON REGARDLESS OF CIRCUMSTANCES.

28 November, 1809

Count von Berchtenwald:

Within the past half hour, that is, at about eleven o'clock tonight, the man calling himself Benjamin Bathurst was shot and killed by a sentry at the Ministry of Police, while attempting to escape from custody.

A sentry on duty in the rear courtyard of the Ministry observed a man attempting to leave the building in a suspicious and furtive manner. This sentry, who was under the strictest orders to allow no one to enter or leave without written authorization, challenged him; when he attempted to run, the sentry fired his musket at him, bringing him down. At the shot, the Sergeant of the Guard rushed into the courtyard with his detail, and the man whom the sentry had shot was found to be the Englishman, Benjamin Bathurst. He had been hit in the chest with an ounce ball, and died before the doctor could arrive, and without recovering consciousness.

An investigation revealed that the prisoner, who was confined on the third floor of the building, had fashioned a rope from his bedding, his bed cord, and the leather strap of his bell pull. This rope was only long enough to reach to the window of the office on the second floor, directly below, but he managed to enter this by kicking the glass out of the window. I am trying to find out how he could do this without being heard. I can assure you that somebody is going to smart for this night's work. As for the sentry, he acted within his orders; I have commended him for doing his duty, and for good shooting, and I assume full responsibility for the death of the prisoner at his hands.

I have no idea why the self-so-called Benjamin Bathurst, who, until now, was well-behaved and seemed to take his confinement philosophically, should suddenly make this rash and fatal attempt, unless it was because of those infernal dunderheads of madhouse doctors who have been bothering him. Only this afternoon they deliberately handed him a bundle of newspapers — Prussian, Austrian, French, and English — all dated within the last month. They wanted they said, to see how he would react. Well, God pardon them, they've found out!

What do you think should be done about giving the body burial?

Krutz

(From the British Minister, to the Count von Berchtenwald.)

December 20th, 1809

My dear Count von Berchtenwald:

Reply from London to my letter of the 28th, which accompanied the dispatch case and the other papers, has finally come to hand. The papers which you wanted returned — the copies of the statements taken at Perleburg, the letter to the Baron von Krutz from the police captain, Hartenstein, and the personal letter of Krutz's nephew, Lieutenant von Tarlburg, and the letter of safe-conduct found in the dispatch case — accompany herewith. I don't know what the people at Whitehall did with the other papers; tossed them into the nearest fire, for my guess. Were I in your place, that's where the papers I am returning would go.

I have heard nothing, yet, from my dispatch of the 29th concerning the death of the man who called himself Benjamin Bathurst, but I doubt very much if any official notice will ever be taken of it. Your government had a perfect right to detain the fellow, and, that being the case, he attempted to escape at his own risk. After all, sentries are not required to carry loaded muskets in order to discourage them from putting their hands in their pockets.

To hazard a purely unofficial opinion, I should not imagine that London is very much dissatisfied with this dénouement. His Majesty's government are a hard-headed and matter-of-fact set of gentry who do not relish mysteries, least of all mysteries whose solution may be more disturbing than the original problem.

This is entirely confidential, but those papers which were in that dispatch case kicked up the devil's own row in London, with half the government bigwigs protesting their innocence to high Heaven, and the rest accusing one another of complicity in the hoax. If that was somebody's intention, it was literally a howling success. For a while, it was even feared that there would be questions in Parliament, but eventually, the whole vexatious business was hushed.

You may tell Count Tarlburg's son that his little friend is a most talented young lady; her sketch was highly commended by no less an authority than Sir Thomas Lawrence, and here comes the most bedeviling part of a thoroughly bedeviled business. The picture was instantly recognized. It is a very fair likeness of Benjamin Bathurst, or, I should say, Sir Benjamin Bathurst, who is King's lieutenant governor for the Crown Colony of Georgia. As Sir Thomas Lawrence did his portrait a few years back, he is in an excellent position to criticize the work of Lieutenant von Tarlburg's young lady. However, Sir Benjamin Bathurst was known to have been in Savannah, attending to the duties of his office, and in the public eye, all the while that his double was in Prussia. Sir Benjamin does not have a twin brother. It has been suggested that this fellow might be a half-brother, but, as far as I know, there is no justification for this theory.

The General Bonaparte, alias the Emperor Napoleon, who is given so much mention in the dispatches, seems also to have a counterpart in actual life; there is, in the French army, a Colonel of Artillery by that name, a Corsican who Gallicized his original name of Napolione Buonaparte. He is a most brilliant military theoretician; I am sure some of your own officers, like General Scharnhorst, could tell you about him. His loyalty to the French monarchy has never been questioned.

This same correspondence to fact seems to crop up everywhere in that amazing collection of pseudo-dispatches and pseudo-State papers.

The United States of America, you will recall, was the style by which the rebellious colonies referred to themselves, in the Declaration of Philadelphia. The James Madison who is mentioned as the current President of the United States is now living, in exile, in Switzerland. His alleged predecessor in office, Thomas Jefferson, was the author of the rebel Declaration; after the defeat of the rebels, he escaped to Havana, and died, several years ago, in the Principality of Lichtenstein.

I was quite amused to find our old friend Cardinal Talleyrand — without the ecclesiastical title — cast in the role of chief adviser to the usurper, Bonaparte. His Eminence, I have always thought, is the sort of fellow who would land on his feet on top of any heap, and who would as little scruple to be Prime Minister to His Satanic Majesty as to His Most Christian Majesty.

I was baffled, however, by one name, frequently mentioned in those fantastic papers. This was the English general, Wellington. I haven't the least idea who this person might be.

I have the honor, your excellency, et cetera, et cetera, et cetera,

Sir Arthur Wellesley

Time and Time Again

*B*linded by the bomb-flash and numbed by the narcotic injection, he could not estimate the extent of his injuries, but he knew that he was dying. Around him, in the darkness, voices sounded as through a thick wall.

"They mighta left mosta these Joes where they was. Half of them won't even last till the truck comes."

"No matter; so long as they're alive, they must be treated," another voice, crisp and cultivated, rebuked. "Better start taking names, while we're waiting."

"Yes, sir." Fingers fumbled at his identity badge. "Hartley, Allan; Captain, G5, Chem. Research AN/73/D. Serial, SO-23869403J."

"Allan Hartley!" The medic officer spoke in shocked surprise. "Why, he's the man who wrote 'Children of the Mist,' 'Rose of Death,' and 'Conqueror's Road'!"

He tried to speak, and must have stirred; the corpsman's voice sharpened.

"Major, I think he's part conscious. Mebbe I better give him 'nother shot."

"Yes, yes; by all means, sergeant."

Something jabbed Allan Hartley in the back of the neck. Soft billows of oblivion closed in upon him, and all that remained to him was a tiny spark of awareness, glowing alone and lost in a great darkness.

*T*he Spark grew brighter. He was more than a something that merely knew that it existed. He was a man, and he had a name, and a military rank, and memories. Memories of the searing blue-green flash, and of what he had been doing outside the shelter the moment before, and memories of the month-long siege, and of the retreat from the north, and memories of the days before the War, back to the time when he had been little Allan Hartley, a schoolboy, the son of a successful lawyer, in Williamsport, Pennsylvania.

His mother he could not remember; there was only a vague impression of the house full of people who had tried to comfort him for something he could not understand. But he remembered the old German woman who had kept house for his father, afterward, and he remembered his bedroom, with its chintz-covered chairs, and the warm-colored patch quilt on the old cherry bed, and the tan curtains at the windows, edged with dusky red, and the morning sun shining through them. He could almost see them, now.

He blinked. He *could* see them!

*F*or a long time, he lay staring at them unbelievingly, and then he deliberately closed his eyes and counted ten seconds, and as he counted, terror gripped him. He was afraid to open them again, lest he find himself blind, or gazing at the filth and wreckage of a blasted city, but when he reached ten, he forced himself to look, and gave a sigh of relief. The sunlit curtains and the sun-gilded mist outside were still there.

He reached out to check one sense against another, feeling the rough monk's cloth and the edging of maroon silk thread. They were tangible as well as visible. Then he saw that the back of his hand was unscarred. There should have been a scar, souvenir of a rough-and-tumble brawl of his cub reporter days. He examined both hands closely. An instant later, he had sat up in bed and thrown off the covers, partially removing his pajamas and inspecting as much of his body as was visible.

It was the smooth body of a little boy.

That was ridiculous. He was a man of forty-three; an army officer, a chemist, once a best-selling novelist. He had been married, and divorced ten years ago. He looked again at his body. It was only twelve years old. Fourteen, at the very oldest. His eyes swept the room, wide with wonder. Every detail was familiar: the flower-splashed chair covers; the table that served as desk and catch-all for his possessions; the dresser, with its mirror stuck full of pictures of aircraft. It was the bedroom of his childhood home. He swung his legs over the edge of the bed. They were six inches too short to reach the floor.

For an instant, the room spun dizzily; and he was in the grip of utter panic, all confidence in the evidence of his senses lost. Was he insane? Or delirious? Or had the bomb really killed him; was this what death was like? What was that thing, about "ye become as little children?" He started to laugh, and his juvenile larynx made giggling sounds. They seemed funny, too, and aggravated his mirth. For a little while, he was on the edge of hysteria and then, when he managed to control his laughter, he felt calmer. If he were dead, then he must be a discarnate entity, and would be able to penetrate matter. To his relief, he was unable to push his hand through the bed. So he was alive; he was also fully awake, and, he hoped, rational. He rose to his feet and prowled about the room, taking stock of its contents.

There was no calendar in sight, and he could find no newspapers or dated periodicals, but he knew that it was prior to July 18, 1946. On that day, his fourteenth birthday, his father had given him a light .22 rifle, and it had been hung on a pair of rustic forks on the wall. It was not there now, nor ever had been. On the table, he saw a boys' book of military aircraft, with a clean, new dustjacket; the flyleaf was inscribed: *To Allan Hartley, from his father, on his thirteenth birthday, 7/18 '45.* Glancing out the window at the foliage on the trees, he estimated the date at late July or early August, 1945; that would make him just thirteen.

His clothes were draped on a chair beside the bed. Stripping off his pajamas, he donned shorts, then sat down and picked up a pair of lemon-colored socks, which he regarded with disfavor. As he pulled one on, a church bell began to clang. St. Boniface, up on the hill, ringing for early Mass; so this was Sunday. He paused, the second sock in his hand.

There was no question that his present environment was actual. Yet, on the other hand, he possessed a set of memories completely at variance with it. Now, suppose, since his environment were not an illusion, everything else were? Suppose all these troublesome memories were no more than a dream? Why, he was just little Allan Hartley, safe in his room on a Sunday morning, badly scared by a nightmare! Too much science fiction, Allan; too many comic books!

That was a wonderfully comforting thought, and he hugged it to him contentedly. It lasted all the while he was buttoning up his shirt and pulling on his pants, but when he reached for his shoes, it evaporated. Ever since he had wakened, he realized, he had been occupied with thoughts utterly incomprehensible to any thirteen-year-old; even thinking in words that would have been so much Sanscrit to himself at thirteen. He shook his head regretfully. The just-a-dream hypothesis went by the deep six.

He picked up the second shoe and glared at it as though it were responsible for his predicament. He was going to have to be careful. An unexpected display of adult characteristics might give rise to some questions he would find hard to answer credibly. Fortunately, he was an only child; there would be no brothers or sisters to trip him up. Old

Mrs. Stauber, the housekeeper, wouldn't be much of a problem; even in his normal childhood, he had bulked like an intellectual giant in comparison to her. But his father —

Now, there the going would be tough. He knew that shrewd attorney's mind, whetted keen on a generation of lying and reluctant witnesses. Sooner or later, he would forget for an instant and betray himself. Then he smiled, remembering the books he had discovered, in his late 'teens, on his father's shelves and recalling the character of the openminded agnostic lawyer. If he could only avoid the inevitable unmasking until he had a plausible explanatory theory.

*B*lake Hartley was leaving the bathroom as Allan Hartley opened his door and stepped into the hall. The lawyer was bare-armed and in slippers; at forty-eight, there was only a faint powdering of grey in his dark hair, and not a grey thread in his clipped mustache. The old Merry Widower, himself, Allan thought, grinning as he remembered the white-haired but still vigorous man from whom he'd parted at the outbreak of the War.

"'Morning, Dad," he greeted.

"'Morning, son. You're up early. Going to Sunday school?"

Now there was the advantage of a father who'd cut his first intellectual tooth on Tom Paine and Bob Ingersoll; attendance at divine services was on a strictly voluntary basis.

"Why, I don't think so; I want to do some reading, this morning."

"That's always a good thing to do," Blake Hartley approved. "After breakfast, suppose you take a walk down to the station and get me a *Times.*" He dug in his trouser pocket and came out with a half dollar. "Get anything you want for yourself, while you're at it."

Allan thanked his father and pocketed the coin.

"Mrs. Stauber'll still be at Mass," he suggested. "Say I get the paper now; breakfast won't be ready till she gets here."

"Good idea." Blake Hartley nodded, pleased. "You'll have three-quarters of an hour, at least."

*S*o far, he congratulated himself, everything had gone smoothly. Finishing his toilet, he went downstairs and onto the street, turning left at Brandon to Campbell, and left again in the direction of the station. Before he reached the underpass, a dozen half-forgotten memories had revived. Here was a house that would, in a few years, be gutted by fire.

Here were four dwellings standing where he had last seen a five-story apartment building. A gasoline station and a weed-grown lot would shortly be replaced by a supermarket. The environs of the station itself were a complete puzzle to him, until he oriented himself.

He bought a New York *Times,* glancing first of all at the date line. Sunday, August 5, 1945; he'd estimated pretty closely. The battle of Okinawa had been won. The Potsdam Conference had just ended. There were still pictures of the B-25 crash against the Empire State Building, a week ago Saturday. And Japan was still being pounded by bombs from the air and shells from off-shore naval guns. Why, tomorrow, Hiroshima was due for the Big Job! It amused him to reflect that he was probably the only person in Williamsport who knew that.

On the way home, a boy, sitting on the top step of a front porch, hailed him. Allan replied cordially, trying to remember who it was. Of course; Larry Morton! He and Allan had been buddies. They probably had been swimming, or playing Commandos and Germans, the afternoon before. Larry had gone to Cornell the same year that Allan had gone to Penn State; they had both graduated in 1954. Larry had gotten into some Government bureau, and then he had married a Pittsburgh girl, and had become twelfth vice-president of her father's firm. He had been killed, in 1968, in a plane crash.

"You gonna Sunday school?" Larry asked, mercifully unaware of the fate Allan foresaw for him.

"Why, no. I have some things I want to do at home." He'd have to watch himself. Larry would spot a difference quicker than any adult. "Heck with it," he added.

"Golly, I wisht I c'ld stay home from Sunday school whenever I wanted to," Larry envied. "How about us goin' swimmin', at the Canoe Club, 'safter?"

Allan thought fast. "Gee, I wisht I c'ld," he replied, lowering his grammatical sights. "I gotta stay home, 'safter. We're expectin' comp'ny; coupla aunts of mine. Dad wants me to stay home when they come."

That went over all right. Anybody knew that there was no rational accounting for the vagaries of the adult mind, and no appeal from adult demands. The prospect of company at the Hartley home would keep Larry away, that afternoon. He showed his disappointment.

"Aw, jeepers creepers!" he blasphemed euphemistically.

"Mebbe t'morrow," Allan said. "If I c'n make it. I gotta go, now; ain't had breakfast yet." He scuffed his feet boyishly, exchanged so-longs with his friend, and continued homeward.

*A*s he had hoped, the Sunday paper kept his father occupied at breakfast, to the exclusion of any dangerous table talk. Blake Hartley was still deep in the financial section when Allan left the table and went to the library. There should be two books there to which he wanted badly to refer. For a while, he was afraid that his father had not acquired them prior to 1945, but he finally found them, and carried them onto the front porch, along with a pencil and a ruled yellow scratch pad. In his experienced future — or his past-to-come — Allan Hartley had been accustomed to doing his thinking with a pencil. As reporter, as novelist plotting his work, as amateur chemist in his home laboratory, as scientific warfare research officer, his ideas had always been clarified by making notes. He pushed a chair to the table and built up the seat with cushions, wondering how soon he would become used to the proportional disparity between himself and the furniture. As he opened the books and took his pencil in his hand, there was one thing missing. If he could only smoke a pipe, now!

His father came out and stretched in a wicker chair with the *Times* book-review section. The morning hours passed. Allan Hartley leafed through one book and then the other. His pencil moved rapidly at times; at others, he doodled absently. There was no question, anymore, in his mind, as to what or who he was. He was Allan Hartley, a man of forty-three, marooned in his own thirteen-year-old body, thirty years back in his own past. That was, of course, against all common sense, but he was easily able to ignore that objection. It had been made before: against the astronomy of Copernicus, and the geography of Columbus, and the biology of Darwin, and the industrial technology of Samuel Colt, and the military doctrines of Charles de Gaulle. Today's common sense had a habit of turning into tomorrow's utter nonsense. What he needed, right now, but bad, was a theory that would explain what had happened to him.

Understanding was beginning to dawn when Mrs. Stauber came out to announce midday dinner.

"I hope you von't mind haffin' it so early," she apologized. "Mein sister, Jennie, offer in Nippenose, she iss sick; I vant to go see her, dis afternoon, yet. I'll be back in blenty time to get supper, Mr. Hartley."

"Hey, Dad!" Allan spoke up. "Why can't we get our own supper, and have a picnic, like? That'd be fun, and Mrs. Stauber could stay as long as she wanted to."

His father looked at him. Such consideration for others was a most gratifying deviation from the juvenile norm; dawn of altruism, or something. He gave hearty assent:

"Why, of course, Mrs. Stauber. Allan and I can shift for ourselves, this evening; can't we, Allan? You needn't come back till tomorrow morning."

"*Ach,* t'ank you! T'ank you so mooch, Mr. Hartley."

At dinner, Allan got out from under the burden of conversation by questioning his father about the War and luring him into a lengthy dissertation on the difficulties of the forthcoming invasion of Japan. In view of what he remembered of the next twenty-four hours, Allan was secretly amused. His father was sure that the War would run on to mid-1946.

After dinner, they returned to the porch, Hartley *père* smoking a cigar and carrying out several law books. He only glanced at these occasionally; for the most part, he sat and blew smoke rings, and watched them float away. Some thrice-guilty felon was about to be triumphantly acquitted by a weeping jury; Allan could recognize a courtroom masterpiece in the process of incubation.

*I*t was several hours later that the crunch of feet on the walk caused father and son to look up simultaneously. The approaching visitor was a tall man in a rumpled black suit; he had knobby wrists and big, awkward hands; black hair flecked with grey, and a harsh, bigoted face. Allan remembered him. Frank Gutchall. Lived on Campbell Street; a religious fanatic, and some sort of lay preacher. Maybe he needed legal advice; Allan could vaguely remember some incident —

"Ah, good afternoon, Mr. Gutchall. Lovely day, isn't it?" Blake Hartley said.

Gutchall cleared his throat. "Mr. Hartley, I wonder if you could lend me a gun and some bullets," he began, embarrassedly. "My little dog's been hurt, and it's suffering something terrible. I want a gun, to put the poor thing out of its pain."

"Why, yes; of course. How would a 20-gauge shotgun do?" Blake Hartley asked. "You wouldn't want anything heavy."

Gutchall fidgeted. "Why, er, I was hoping you'd let me have a little gun." He held his hands about six inches apart. "A pistol, that I could put in my pocket. It wouldn't look right, to carry a hunting gun on the Lord's day; people wouldn't understand that it was for a work of mercy."

The lawyer nodded. In view of Gutchall's religious beliefs, the objection made sense.

"Well, I have a Colt .38-special," he said, "but you know, I belong to this Auxiliary Police outfit. If I were called out for duty, this evening, I'd need it. How soon could you bring it back?"

Something clicked in Allan Hartley's mind. He remembered, now, what that incident had been. He knew, too, what he had to do.

"Dad, aren't there some cartridges left for the Luger?" he asked.

Blake Hartley snapped his fingers. "By George, yes! I have a German automatic I can let you have, but I wish you'd bring it back as soon as possible. I'll get it for you."

Before he could rise, Allan was on his feet.

"Sit still, Dad; I'll get it. I know where the cartridges are." With that, he darted into the house and upstairs.

The Luger hung on the wall over his father's bed. Getting it down, he dismounted it, working with rapid precision. He used the blade of his pocketknife to unlock the endpiece of the breechblock, slipping out the firing pin and buttoning it into his shirt pocket. Then he reassembled the harmless pistol, and filled the clip with 9-millimeter cartridges from the bureau drawer.

There was an extension telephone beside the bed. Finding Gutchall's address in the directory, he lifted the telephone, and stretched his handkerchief over the mouthpiece. Then he dialed Police Headquarters.

"This is Blake Hartley," he lied, deepening his voice and copying his father's tone. "Frank Gutchall, who lives at. . .take this down" — he gave Gutchall's address — "has just borrowed a pistol from me, ostensibly to shoot a dog. He has no dog. He intends shooting his wife. Don't argue about how I know; there isn't time. Just take it for granted that I do. I disabled the pistol — took out the firing pin — but if he finds out what I did, he may get some other weapon. He's on his way home, but he's on foot. If you hurry, you may get a man there before he arrives, and grab him before he finds out the pistol won't shoot."

"O. K., Mr. Hartley. We'll take care of it. Thanks."

"And I wish you'd get my pistol back, as soon as you can. It's something I brought home from the other War, and I shouldn't like to lose it."

"We'll take care of that, too. Thank you, Mr. Hartley."

He hung up, and carried the Luger and the loaded clip down to the porch.

"*L*ook, Mr. Gutchall; here's how it works," he said, showing it to the visitor. Then he slapped in the clip and yanked up on the toggle loading the chamber. "It's ready to shoot, now; this is the safety." He pushed it on. "When you're ready to shoot, just shove it forward and up, and then pull the trigger. You have to pull the trigger each time; it's loaded for eight shots. And be sure to put the safety back when you're through shooting."

"Did you load the chamber?" Blake Hartley demanded.

"Sure. It's on safe, now."

"Let me see." His father took the pistol, being careful to keep his finger out of the trigger guard, and looked at it. "Yes, that's all right." He repeated the instructions Allan had given, stressing the importance of putting the safety on after using. "Understand how it works, now?" he asked.

"Yes, I understand how it works. Thank you, Mr. Hartley. Thank you, too, young man."

Gutchall put the Luger in his hip pocket, made sure it wouldn't fall out, and took his departure.

"You shouldn't have loaded it," Hartley *père* reproved, when he was gone.

Allan sighed. This was it; the masquerade was over.

"I had to, to keep you from fooling with it," he said. "I didn't want you finding out that I'd taken out the firing pin."

"You what?"

"Gutchall didn't want that gun to shoot a dog. He has no dog. He meant to shoot his wife with it. He's a religious maniac; sees visions, hears voices, receives revelations, talks with the Holy Ghost. The Holy Ghost probably put him up to this caper. I'll submit that any man who holds long conversations with the Deity isn't to be trusted with a gun, and neither is any man who lies about why he wants one. And while I was at it, I called the police, on the upstairs phone. I had to use your name; I deepened my voice and talked through a handkerchief."

"You —" Blake Hartley jumped as though bee-stung. "Why did you have to do that?"

"You know why. I couldn't have told them, 'This is little Allan Hartley, just thirteen years old; please, Mr. Policeman, go and arrest Frank Gutchall before he goes root-toot-toot at his wife with my pappa's Luger.' That would have gone over big, now, wouldn't it?"

"And suppose he really wants to shoot a dog; what sort of a mess will I be in?"

"No mess at all. If I'm wrong — which I'm not — I'll take the thump for it, myself. It'll pass for a dumb kid trick, and nothing'll be done. But if I'm right, you'll have to front for me. They'll keep your name out of it, but they'd give me a lot of cheap boy-hero publicity, which I don't want." He picked up his pencil again. "We should have the complete returns in about twenty minutes."

*T*hat was a ten-minute under-estimate, and it was another quarter-hour before the detective-sergeant who returned the Luger had finished congratulating Blake Hartley and giving him the thanks of the Department. After he had gone, the lawyer picked up the Luger, withdrew the clip, and ejected the round in the chamber.

"Well," he told his son, "you were right. You saved that woman's life." He looked at the automatic, and then handed it across the table. "Now, let's see you put that firing pin back."

Allan Hartley dismantled the weapon, inserted the missing part, and put it together again, then snapped it experimentally and returned it to his father. Blake Hartley looked at it again, and laid it on the table.

"Now, son, suppose we have a little talk," he said softly.

"But I explained everything." Allan objected innocently.

"You did not," his father retorted. "Yesterday you'd never have thought of a trick like this; why, you wouldn't even have known how to take this pistol apart. And at dinner, I caught you using language and expressing ideas that were entirely outside anything you'd ever known before. Now, I want to know — and I mean this literally."

Allan chuckled. "I hope you're not toying with the rather medieval notion of obsession," he said.

Blake Hartley started. Something very like that must have been flitting through his mind. He opened his mouth to say something, then closed it abruptly.

"The trouble is, I'm not sure you aren't right," his son continued. "You say you find me — changed. When did you first notice a difference?"

"Last night, you were still my little boy. This morning —" Blake Hartley was talking more to himself than to Allan. "I don't know. You were unusually silent at breakfast. And come to think of it, there was something . . . something strange . . . about you when I saw you in the hall, upstairs. . . . Allan!" he burst out, vehemently. "What has happened to you?"

Allan Hartley felt a twinge of pain. What his father was going through was almost what he, himself, had endured, in the first few minutes after waking.

"I wish I could be sure, myself, Dad," he said. "You see, when I woke, this morning, I hadn't the least recollection of anything I'd done yesterday. August 4, 1945, that is," he specified. "I was positively convinced that I was a man of forty-three, and my last memory was of lying on a stretcher, injured by a bomb explosion. And I was equally convinced that this had happened in 1975."

"Huh?" His father straightened. "Did you say nineteen *seventy*-five?" He thought for a moment. "That's right; in 1975, you will be forty-three. A bomb, you say?"

Allan nodded. "During the siege of Buffalo, in the Third World War," he said, "I was a captain in G5 — Scientific Warfare, General Staff. There'd been a transpolar air invasion of Canada, and I'd been sent to the front to check on service failures of a new lubricating oil for combat equipment. A week after I got there, Ottawa fell, and the retreat started. We made a stand at Buffalo, and that was where I copped it. I remember being picked up, and getting a narcotic injection. The next thing I knew, I was in bed, upstairs, and it was 1945 again, and I was back in my own little thirteen-year-old body."

"Oh, Allan, you just had a nightmare to end nightmares!" his father assured him, laughing a trifle too heartily. "That's all!"

"That was one of the first things I thought of. I had to reject it; it just wouldn't fit the facts. Look; a normal dream is part of the dreamer's own physical brain, isn't it? Well, here is a part about two thousand percent greater than the whole from which it was taken. Which is absurd."

"You mean all this Battle of Buffalo stuff? That's easy. All the radio commentators have been harping on the horrors of World War III, and you couldn't have avoided hearing some of it. You just have an undigested chunk of H. V. Kaltenborn raising hell in your subconscious."

"It wasn't just World War III; it was everything. My four years at high school, and my four years at Penn State, and my seven years as a reporter on the Philadelphia Record. And my novels: 'Children of the Mist,' 'Rose of Death,' 'Conqueror's Road.' They were no kid stuff. Why, yesterday I'd never even have thought of some of the ideas I used in my detective stories, that I published under a *nom-de-plume*. And my hobby, chemistry; I was pretty good at that. Patented a couple of processes that made me as much money as my writing. You think a thirteen-year-old just dreamed all that up? Or, here; you speak French, don't you?" He switched languages and spoke at some length in good conversational slang-spiced Parisian. "Too bad you don't speak Spanish, too," he added, reverting to English. "Except for a Mexican accent you could cut with a machete, I'm even better there than in French. And I know some German, and a little Russian."

*B*lake Hartley was staring at his son, stunned. It was some time before he could make himself speak.

"I could barely keep up with you, in French," he admitted. "I can swear that in the last thirteen years of your life, you had absolutely no chance to learn it. All right; you lived till 1975, you say. Then, all of a sudden, you found yourself back here, thirteen years old, in 1945. I suppose you remember everything in between?" he asked. "Did you ever read James Branch Cabell? Remember Florian de Puysange, in 'The High Place'?"

"Yes. You find the same idea in 'Jurgen' too," Allan said. "You know, I'm beginning to wonder if Cabell mightn't have known something he didn't want to write."

"But it's impossible!" Blake Hartley hit the table with his hand, so hard that the heavy pistol bounced. The loose round he had ejected from the chamber toppled over and started to roll, falling off the edge. He stooped and picked it up. "How can you go back, against time? And the time you claim you came from doesn't exist, now; it hasn't happened yet." He reached for the pistol magazine, to insert the cartridge, and as he did, he saw the books in front of his son. "Dunne's 'Experiment with Time,'" he commented. "And J. N. M. Tyrrell's 'Science and Psychical Phenomena.' Are you trying to work out a theory?"

"Yes." It encouraged Allan to see that his father had unconsciously adopted an adult-to-adult manner. "I think I'm getting somewhere, too. You've read these books? Well, look, Dad; what's your attitude on precognition? The ability of the human mind to exhibit real knowledge, apart from logical inference, of future events? You think Dunne is telling the truth about his experiences? Or that the cases in Tyrrell's book are properly verified, and can't be explained away on the basis of chance?"

Blake Hartley frowned. "I don't know," he confessed. "The evidence is the sort that any court in the world would accept, if it concerned ordinary, normal events. Especially the cases investigated by the Society for Psychical Research: they *have* been verified. But how can anybody know of something that hasn't happened yet? If it hasn't happened yet, it doesn't exist, and you can't have real knowledge of something that has no real existence."

"Tyrrell discusses that dilemma, and doesn't dispose of it. I think I can. If somebody has real knowledge of the future, then the future must be available to the present mind. And if any moment other than the bare present exists, then all time must be totally present; every moment must be perpetually coexistent with every other moment," Allan said.

"Yes. I think I see what you mean. That was Dunne's idea, wasn't it?"

"No. Dunne postulated an infinite series of time dimensions, the entire extent of each being the bare present moment of the next. What I'm postulating is the perpetual coexistence of every moment of time in this dimension, just as every graduation on a yardstick exists equally with every other graduation, but each at a different point in space."

"Well, as far as duration and sequence go, that's all right," the father agreed. "But how about the 'Passage of Time'?"

"Well, time *does* appear to pass. So does the landscape you see from a moving car window. I'll suggest that both are illusions of the same kind. We imagine time to be dynamic, because we've never viewed it from a fixed point, but if it is totally present, then it must be static, and in that case, we're moving through time."

"That seems all right. But what's your car window?"

"If all time is totally present, then you must exist simultaneously at every moment along your individual life span," Allan said. "Your physical body, and your mind, and all the thoughts contained in your mind, each at its appropriate moment in sequence. But what is it that exists only at the bare moment we think of as *now?*"

*B*lake Hartley grinned. Already, he was accepting his small son as an intellectual equal.

"Please, teacher; what?"

"Your consciousness. And don't say, 'What's that?' Teacher doesn't know. But we're only conscious of one moment; the illusory now. This is 'now,' and it was 'now' when you asked that question, and it'll be 'now' when I stop talking, but each is a different moment. We imagine that all those nows are rushing past us. Really, they're standing still, and our consciousness is whizzing past them."

His father thought that over for some time. Then he sat up. "Hey!" he cried, suddenly. "If some part of our ego is time-free and passes from moment to moment, it must be extraphysical, because the physical body exists at every moment through which the consciousness passes. And if it's extraphysical, there's no reason whatever for assuming that it passes out of existence when it reaches the moment of the death of the body. Why, there's logical evidence for survival, independent of any alleged spirit communication! You can toss out Patience Worth, and Mrs. Osborne Leonard's Feda, and Sir Oliver Lodge's son, and Wilfred Brandon, and all the other spirit-communicators, and you still have evidence."

"I hadn't thought of that," Allan confessed. "I think you're right. Well, let's put that at the bottom of the agenda and get on with this time business. You 'lose consciousness' as in sleep; where does your consciousness go? I think it simply detaches from the moment at which you go to sleep, and moves backward or forward along the line of moment-sequence, to some prior or subsequent moment, attaching there."

"Well, why don't we know anything about that?" Blake Hartley asked. "It never seems to happen. We go to sleep tonight, and it's always tomorrow morning when we wake; never day-before-yesterday, or last month, or next year."

"It never . . . or almost never . . . *seems* to happen; you're right there. Know why? Because if the consciousness goes forward, it attaches at a moment when the physical brain contains memories of the previous, consciously unexperienced, moment. You wake, remembering the evening before, because that's the memory contained in your mind at that moment, and back of it are memories of all the events in the interim. See?"

"Yes. But how about backward movement, like this experience of yours?"

"This experience of mine may not be unique, but I never heard of another case like it. What usually happens is that the memories carried back by the consciousness are buried in the subconscious mind. You know how thick the wall between the subconscious and the conscious mind is. These dreams of Dunne's, and the cases in Tyrrell's book, are leakage. That's why precognitions are usually incomplete and distorted, and generally trivial. The wonder isn't that good cases are so few; it's surprising that there are any at all." Allan looked at the papers in front of him. "I haven't begun to theorize about how I managed to remember everything. It may have been the radiations from the bomb, or the effect of the narcotic, or both together, or something at this end, or a combination of all three. But the fact remains that my subconscious barrier didn't function, and everything got through. So, you see, I am obsessed — by my own future identity."

"And I'd been afraid that you'd been, well, taken-over by some . . . some outsider." Blake Hartley grinned weakly. "I don't mind admitting, Allan, that what's happened has been a shock. But that other . . . I just couldn't have taken that."

"No. Not and stayed sane. But really, I am your son; the same entity I was yesterday. I've just had what you might call an educational short cut."

"I'll say you have!" His father laughed in real amusement. He discovered that his cigar had gone out, and re-lit it. "Here; if you can remember the next thirty years, suppose you tell me when the War's going to end. This one, I mean."

"The Japanese surrender will be announced at exactly 1901 — 7:01 P. M. present style — on August 14. A week from Tuesday. Better make sure we have plenty of grub in the house by then. Everything will be closed up tight till Thursday morning; even the restaurants. I remember, we had nothing to eat in the house but some scraps."

"Well! It is handy, having a prophet in the family! I'll see to it Mrs. Stauber gets plenty of groceries in. . . . Tuesday a week? That's pretty sudden, isn't it?"

"The Japs are going to think so," Allan replied. He went on to describe what was going to happen.

His father swore softly. "You know, I've heard talk about atomic energy, but I thought it was just Buck Rogers stuff. Was that the sort of bomb that got you?"

"That was a firecracker to the bomb that got me. That thing exploded a good ten miles away."

Blake Hartley whistled softly. "And that's going to happen in thirty years! You know, son, if I were you, I wouldn't like to have to know about a thing like that." He looked at Allan for a moment. "Please, if you know, don't ever tell me when I'm going to die."

Allan smiled. "I can't. I had a letter from you just before I left for the front. You were seventy-eight, then, and you were still hunting, and fishing, and flying your own plane. But I'm not going to get killed in any Battle of Buffalo, this time, and if I can prevent it, and I think I can, there won't be any World War III."

"But — You say all time exists, perpetually coexistent and totally present," his father said. "Then it's right there in front of you, and you're getting closer to it, every watch tick."

Allan Hartley shook his head. "You know what I remembered, when Frank Gutchall came to borrow a gun?" he asked. "Well, the other time, I hadn't been home: I'd been swimming at the Canoe Club, with Larry Morton. When I got home, about half an hour from now, I found the house full of cops. Gutchall talked the .38 officers' model out of you, and gone home; he'd shot his wife four times through the body, finished her off with another one back of the ear, and then used his sixth shot to blast his brains out. The cops traced the gun; they took a very poor view of your lending it to him. You never got it back."

"Trust that gang to keep a good gun," the lawyer said.

"I didn't want us to lose it, this time, and I didn't want to see you lose face around City Hall. Gutchalls, of course, are expendable," Allan said. "But my main reason for fixing Frank Gutchall up with a padded cell was that I wanted to know whether or not the future could be altered. I have it on experimental authority that it can be. There must be additional dimensions of time; lines of alternate probabilities. Something like William Seabrook's witch-doctor friend's Fan-Shaped *Destiny.* When I brought memories of the future back to the present, I added certain factors to the causal chain. That set up an entirely new line of probabilities. On no notice at all, I stopped a murder and a suicide. With thirty years to work, I can stop a world war. I'll have the means to do it, too."

"The means?"

"Unlimited wealth and influence. Here." Allan picked up a sheet and handed it to his father. "Used properly, we can make two or three million on that, alone. A list of all the Kentucky Derby, Preakness, and Belmont winners to 1970. That'll furnish us primary capital. Then, remember, I was something of a chemist. I took it up, originally, to get background material for one of my detective stories; it fascinated me, and I made it a hobby, and then a source of income. I'm thirty years ahead of any chemist in the world, now. You remember *I. G. Farbenindustrie?* Ten years from now, we'll make them look like pikers."

His father looked at the yellow sheet. "Assault, at eight to one," he said. "I can scrape up about five thousand for that — Yes; in ten years — Any other little operations you have in mind?" he asked.

"About 1950, we start building a political organization, here in Pennsylvania. In 1960, I think we can elect you President. The world situation will be crucial, by that time, and we had a good-natured nonentity in the White House then, who let things go till war became inevitable. I think President Hartley can be trusted to take a strong line of policy. In the meantime, you can read Machiavelli."

"That's my little boy, talking!"

Blake Hartley said softly. "All right, son; I'll do just what you tell me, and when you grow up, I'll be president. . . . Let's go get supper, now."

The Return

by H. Beam Piper
and
John J. McGuire

Altamont cast a quick, routine, glance at the instrument panels and then looked down through the transparent nose of the helicopter at the yellow-brown river five hundred feet below. Next he scraped the last morsel from his plate and ate it.

"What did you make this out of, Jim?" he asked. "I hope you kept notes, while you were concocting it. It's good."

"The two smoked pork chops left over from yesterday evening," Loudons said, "and that bowl of rice that's been taking up space in the refrigerator the last couple of days together with a little egg powder, and some milk. I ground the chops up and mixed them with the rice and the other stuff. Then added some bacon, to make grease to fry it in."

Altamont chuckled. That was Loudons, all right; he could take a few leftovers, mess them together, pop them in the skillet, and have a meal that would turn the chef back at the Fort green with envy. He filled his cup and offered the pot.

"Caffchoc?" he asked.

Loudons held his cup out to be filled, blew on it, sipped, and then hunted on the ledge under the desk for the butt of the cigar he had half-smoked the evening before.

"Did you ever drink coffee, Monty?" the socio-psychologist asked, getting the cigar drawing to his taste.

"Coffee? No. I've read about it, of course. We'll have to organize an expedition to Brazil, some time, to get seeds, and try raising some."

Loudons blew a smoke ring toward the rear of the cabin.

"A much overrated beverage," he replied. "We found some, once, when I was on that expedition into Idaho, in what must have been the stockroom of a hotel. Vacuum-packed in moisture-proof containers, and free from radioactivity. It wasn't nearly as good as caffchoc. But then, I suppose, a pre-bustup coffee drinker couldn't stomach this stuff we're drinking." He looked forward, up the river they were following. "Get anything on the radio?" he asked. "I noticed you took us up to about ten thousand, while I was shaving."

Altamont got out his pipe and tobacco pouch, filling the former slowly and carefully.

"Not a whisper. I tried Colony Three, in the Ozarks, and I tried to call in that tribe of workers in Louisiana; I couldn't get either."

"Maybe if we tried to get a little more power on the set —"

That was Loudons, too, Altamont thought. There wasn't a better man at the Fort, when it came to dealing with people, but confront him with a problem about things, and he was lost. That was one of the reasons why he and the stocky, phlegmatic social scientist made such a good team, he thought. As far as he, himself, was concerned, people were just a mysterious, exasperatingly unpredictable, order of things which were subject to no known natural laws. That was about the way Loudons thought of things; he couldn't psychoanalyze them.

He gestured with his pipe toward the nuclear-electric conversion unit, between the control-cabin and the living quarters in the rear of the box-car-sized helicopter.

"We have enough power back there to keep this windmill in the air twenty-four hours a day, three hundred and sixty-five days a year, for the next fifteen years," he said. "We just don't have enough radio. If I'd step up the power on this set anymore, it'd burn out before I could say, 'Altamont calling Fort Ridgeway.'"

"How far are we from Pittsburgh, now?" Loudons wanted to know.

Altamont looked across the cabin at the big map of the United States, with its red and green and blue and yellow patchwork of vanished political divisions, and the transparent overlay on which they had plotted their course. The red line started at Fort Ridgeway, in what had once been Arizona It angled east by a little north, to Colony Three, in northern Arkansas; then sharply northeast to St. Louis and its lifeless ruins; then Chicago and Gary, where little bands of Stone Age reversions stalked and fought and ate each other; Detroit, where things that had completely forgotten that they were human emerged from their burrows only at night; Cleveland, where a couple of cobalt bombs must have landed in the lake and drenched everything with radioactivity that still lingered after two centuries; Akron, where vegetation was only beginning to break through the glassy slag; Cincinnati, where they had last stopped —

"How's the leg, this morning, Jim?" he asked.

"Little stiff. Doesn't hurt much, though."

"Why, we're about fifty miles, as we follow the river, and that's relatively straight." He looked down through the transparent nose of the 'copter at a town, now choked with trees that grew among tumbled walls. "I think that's Aliquippa."

Loudons looked and shrugged, then looked again and pointed.

"There's a bear. Just ducked into that church or movie theater or whatever. I wonder what he thinks we are."

Altamont puffed slowly at his pipe, "I wonder if we're going to find anything at all in Pittsburgh."

"You mean people, as distinct from those biped beasts we've found so far? I doubt it," Loudons replied, finishing his caffchoc and wiping his mustache on the back of his hand. "I think the whole eastern half of the country is nothing but forest like this, and the highest type of life is just about three cuts below *Homo Neanderthalensis*, almost impossible to contact, and even more impossible to educate."

"I wasn't thinking about that; I've just about given up hope of finding anybody or even a reasonably high level of barbarism," Altamont said. "I was thinking about that cache of microfilmed books that was buried at the Carnegie Library."

"If it was buried," Loudons qualified. "All we have is that article in that two-century-old copy of *Time* about how the people at the library had constructed the crypt and were beginning the microfilming. We don't know if they ever had a chance to get it finished, before the rockets started landing."

They passed over a dam of flotsam that had banked up at a wrecked bridge and accumulated enough mass to resist the periodic floods that had kept the river usually clear. Three human figures fled across a sand-flat at one end of it and disappeared into the woods; two of them carried spears tipped with something that sparkled in the sunlight, probably shards of glass.

"You know, Monty, I get nightmares, sometimes, about what things must be like in Europe," Loudons said.

Five or six wild cows went crashing through the brush below. Altamont nodded when he saw them.

"Maybe tomorrow, we'll let down and shoot a cow," he said. "I was looking in the freezer-locker; the fresh meat's getting a little low. Or a wild pig, if we find a good stand of oak trees. I could enjoy what you'd do with some acorn-fed pork. Finished?" he asked Loudons. "Take over, then; I'll go back and wash the dishes."

They rose, and Loudons, favoring his left leg, moved over to the seat at the controls. Altamont gathered up the two cups, the stainless-steel dishes, and the knives and forks and spoons, going up the steps over the shielded converter and ducking his head to avoid the seat in the forward top machine-gun turret. He washed and dried the dishes, noting with satisfaction that the gauge of the water tank was still reasonably high, and glanced out one of the windows. Loudons was taking the big helicopter upstairs, for a better view.

Now and then, among the trees, there would be a glint of glassy slag, usually in a fairly small circle. That was to be expected; beside the three or four H-bombs that had fallen on the Pittsburgh area, mentioned in the transcripts of the last news to reach the Fort from outside, the whole district had been pelted, more or less at random, with fission bombs. West of the confluence of the Allegheny and Monongahela, it would probably be worse than this.

"Can you see Pittsburgh yet, Jim?" he called out.

"Yes; it's a mess! Worse than Gary; worse than Akron, even. *Monty!* Come here! I think I have something!"

Picking up the pipe he had laid down, Altamont hurried forward, dodging his six-foot length under the gun turret and swinging down from the walkway over the converter.

"What is it?" he asked.

"Smoke. A lot of smoke, twenty or thirty fires, at the very least." Loudons had shifted from *Forward* to *Hover,* and was peering through a pair of binoculars. "See that island, the long one? Across the river from it, on the north side, toward this end. Yes, by Einstein! And I can see cleared ground, and what I think are houses, inside a stockade —"

*M*urray Hughes walked around the corner of the cabin, into the morning sunlight, lacing his trousers, with his hunting shirt thrown over his bare shoulders, and found, without much surprise, that his father had also slept late. Verner Hughes was just beginning to shave. Inside the kitchen, his mother and the girls were clattering pots and skillets; his younger brother, Hector, was noisily chopping wood. Going through the door, he filled another of the light-metal basins with hot water, found his razor, and went outside again, setting the basin on the bench.

Most of the ware in the Hughes cabin was of light-metal; Murray and his father had mined it in the dead city up the river, from a place where it had floated to the top of a puddle of slag, back when the city had been blasted, at the end of the Old Times. It had been hard work, but the stuff had been easy to carry down to where they had hidden their boat, and, for once, they'd had no trouble with the Scowrers. Too bad they couldn't say as much for yesterday's hunting trip!

As he rubbed lather into the stubble on his face, he cursed with irritation. That had been a bad-luck hunt, all around. They'd gone out before dawn, hunting into the hills to the north, they'd spent all day at it, and shot one small wild pig. Lucky it was small, at that. They'd have had to abandon a full-grown one, after the Scowrers began hunting them. Six of them, as big a band as he'd ever seen together at one time, and they'd gotten between them and the stockade and forced them to circle miles out of their way. His father had shot one, and he'd had to leave his hatchet sticking in the skull of another, when his rifle had misfired.

That meant a trip to the gunsmith's, for a new hatchet and to have the mainspring of the rifle replaced. Nobody could afford to have a rifle that couldn't be trusted, least of all a hunter and prospector. And he'd had words with Alex Barrett, the gunsmith, just the other day. Not that Barrett wouldn't be more than glad to do business with him, once he saw that hard tool-steel he'd dug out of that place down the river. Hardest steel he'd ever found, and hadn't been atom-spoiled, either.

He cleaned, wiped and stropped his razor and put it back in the case; he threw out the wash-water on the compost-pile, and went into the cabin, putting on his shirt and his belt, and passed on through to the front porch, where his father was already eating at the table. The people of the Toon liked to eat in the open; it was something they'd always done, just as they'd always liked to eat together in the evenings.

He sweetened his mug of chicory with a lump of maple sugar and began to sip it before he sat down, standing with one foot on the bench and looking down across the parade ground, past the Aitch-Cue House, toward the river and the wall.

"If you're coming around to Alex's way of thinking — and mine — it won't hurt you to admit it, son," his father said.

He turned, looking at his father with the beginning of anger, and then grinned. The elders were constantly keeping the young men alert with these tests. He checked back over his actions since he had come out onto the porch.

To the table, sugar in his chicory, one foot on the bench, which had reminded him again of the absence of the hatchet from his belt and brought an automatic frown. Then the glance toward the gunsmith's shop, and across the parade ground, at the houses into which so much labor had gone; the wall that had been built from rubble and topped with pointed stakes; the white slabs of marble from the ruined building that marked the graves of the First Tenant and the men of the Old Toon. He *had* thought, in that moment, that maybe his father and Alex Barrett and Reader Rawson and Tenant Mycroft Jones and the others were right — there were too many things here that could not be moved along with them, if they decided to move.

It would be false modesty, refusal to see things as they were, not to admit that he was the leader of the younger men, and the boys of the Irregulars. And last winter, the usual theological arguments about the proper chronological order of the Sacred Books and the true nature of the Risen One had been replaced by a violent controversy when Sholto Jiminez and Birdy Edwards had reopened the old question of the advisability of moving the Toon and settling elsewhere. He'd been in favor of the idea himself, but, for the last month or so, he had begun to doubt the wisdom of it. It was probably reluctance to admit this to himself that had brought on the strained feelings between himself and his old friend the gunsmith.

"I'll have to drill the Irregulars, today," he said. "Birdy Edwards has been drilling them, while we've been hunting. But I'll go up and see Alex about a new hatchet and fixing my rifle. I'll have a talk with him."

He stepped forward to the edge of the porch, still munching on a honey-dipped piece of corn bread, and glanced up at the sky. That was a queer bird; he'd never seen a bird with a wing action like that. Then he realized that the object was not a bird at all.

His father was staring at it, too.

"Murray! That's . . . that's like the old stories from the time of the wars!"

But Murray was already racing across the parade ground toward the Aitch-Cue House, where the big iron ring hung by its chain from a gallowslike post, with the hammer beside it.

*T*he stockaded village grew larger, details became plainer, as the helicopter came slanting down and began spiraling around it. It was a fairly big place, some forty or fifty acres in a rough parallelogram, surrounded by a wall of varicolored stone and brick and concrete rubble from old ruins, topped with a palisade of pointed poles. There was a small jetty projecting out into the river, to which six or eight boats of different sorts were tied; a gate opened onto this from the wall. Inside the stockade, there were close to a hundred buildings, ranging from small cabins to a structure with a belfry, which seemed to have been a church, partly ruined in the war of two centuries ago and later rebuilt. A stream came down from the woods, across the cultivated land around the fortified village; there was a rough flume which carried the water from a dam close to the edge of the forest and provided a fall to turn a mill wheel.

"Look; strip-farming," Loudons pointed. "See the alternate strips of grass and plowed ground. Those people understand soil conservation. They have horses, too."

As he spoke, three riders left the village at a gallop, through a gate on the far side. They separated, and the people in the fields, who had all started for the village, turned and began hurrying toward the woods. Two of the riders headed for a pasture in which cattle had been grazing, and started herding them, also, into the woods. For a while, there was a scurrying of little figures in the village below, and then not a moving thing was in sight.

"There's good organization," Loudons said. "Everybody seems to know what to do, and how to get it done promptly. And look how neat the whole place is. Policed up. I'll bet anything we'll find that they have a military organization, or a military tradition at least. We'll have to find out; you can't understand a people till you understand their background and their social organization."

"Humph. Let me have a look at their artifacts; that'll tell what kind of people they are," Altamont said, swinging his glasses back and forth over the enclosure. "Water-power mill, water-power sawmill — building on the left side of the water wheel; see the pile of fresh lumber beside it. Blacksmith shop, and from that chimney I'd say a small foundry, too. Wonder what that little building out on the tip of the island is; it has a water wheel. Undershot wheel, and it looks as though it could be raised or lowered. But the building's too small for a grist mill. Now, I wonder —"

"Monty, I think we ought to land right in the middle of the enclosure, on that open plaza thing, in front of that building that looks like a reconditioned church. That's probably the Royal Palace, or the Pentagon, or the Kremlin, or whatever."

Altamont started to object, paused, and then nodded. "I think you're right, Jim. From the way they scattered, and got their livestock into the woods, they probably expect us to bomb them. We have to get inside; that's the quickest way to do it." He thought for a moment. "We'd better be armed, when we go out. Pistols, auto-carbines, and a few of those concussion-grenades in case we have to break up a concerted attack. I'll get them."

The plaza and the houses and cabins around it, and the two-hundred-year-old church, were silent and, apparently, lifeless as they set the helicopter down. Once Loudons caught a movement inside the door of a house, and saw a metallic glint. Altamont pointed up at the belfry.

"There's a gun up there," he said. "Looks like about a four-pounder. Brass. I knew that smith-shop was also a foundry. See that little curl of smoke? That's the gunner's slow-match. I'd thought maybe that thing on the island was a powder mill. That would be where they'd put it. Probably extract their niter from the dung of their horses and cows. Sulfur probably from coal-mine drainage. Jim, this is really something!"

"I hope they don't cut loose on us with that thing," Loudons said, looking apprehensively at the brass-rimmed black muzzle that was covering them from the belfry. "I wonder if we ought to — Oh-oh, here they come!"

*T*hree or four young men stepped out of the wide door of the old church. They wore fringed buckskin trousers and buckskin shirts and odd caps of deerskin with visors to shade their eyes and similar beaks behind to protect the neck. They had powder horns and bullet pouches slung over their shoulders, and long rifles in their hands. They stepped aside as soon as they were out; carefully avoiding any gesture of menace, they stood watching the helicopter which had landed among them.

Three other men followed them out; they, too, wore buckskins, and the odd double-visored caps. One had a close-cropped white beard, and on the shoulders of his buckskin shirt he wore the single silver bars of a first lieutenant of the vanished United States Army. He had a pistol on his belt; it had the saw-handle grip of an automatic, but it was a flintlock, as were the rifles of the young men who stood watchfully on either side of the two middle-aged men who accompanied him. The whole party advanced toward the helicopter.

"All right; come on, Monty." Loudons opened the door and let down the steps. Picking up an auto-carbine, he slung it and stepped out of the helicopter, Altamont behind him. They advanced to meet the party from the old church, halting when they were about twenty feet apart.

"I must apologize, lieutenant, for dropping in on you so unceremoniously." He stopped, wondering if the man with the white beard understood a word of what he was saying.

"The natural way to come in, when you travel in the air," the old man replied. "At least, you came in openly. I can promise you a better reception than you got at that city to the west of us a couple of days ago."

"Now how did you know we'd had trouble at Cincinnati day-before-yesterday?" Loudons demanded.

The old man's eyes sparkled with childlike pleasure. "That surprises you, my dear sir? In a moment, I daresay you'll be amazed at the simplicity of it. You have a nasty rip in the left leg of your trousers, and the cloth around it is stained with blood. Through the rip, I perceive a bandage. Obviously, you have suffered a recent wound. I further observe that the side of your flying machine bears recent scratches, as though from the spears or throwing-hatchets of the Scowrers. Evidently they attacked you as you were leaving it; it is fortunate that these cannibal devils are too stupid and too anxious for human flesh to exercise patience."

"Well, that explains how you knew we'd been recently attacked," Loudons told him. "But how did you guess that it had been to the west of here, in a ruined city?"

"I never guess," the oldster with the silver bar and the keystone-shaped red patch on his left shoulder replied. "It is a shocking habit — destructive to the logical faculty. What seems strange to you is only so because you do not follow my train of thought. For example, the wheels and their framework under your flying machine are splashed with mud which seems to be predominantly brick-dust, mixed with plaster. Obviously, you landed recently in a dead city, either during or after a rain. There was a rain here yesterday evening, the wind being from the west. Obviously, you followed behind the rain as it came up the river. And now that I look at your boots, I see traces of the same sort of mud, around the soles and in front of the heels. But this is heartless of us, keeping you standing here on a wounded leg, sir. Come in, and let our medic look at it."

"Well, thank you, lieutenant," Loudons replied. "But don't bother your medic; I've attended to the wound myself, and it wasn't serious to begin with."

"You are a doctor?" the white-bearded man asked.

"Of sorts. A sort of general scientist. My name is Loudons. My friend, Mr. Altamont, here, is a scientist, also."

There was an immediate reaction; all three of the elders of the village, and the young riflemen who had accompanied them, exchanged glances of surprise. Loudons dropped his hand to the grip of his slung auto-carbine, and Altamont sidled unobtrusively away from him, his hand moving as by accident toward the butt of his pistol. The same thought was in both men's minds, that these people might feel, as a heritage of the war of two centuries ago, a hostility to science and scientists. There was no hostility, however, in their manner as the old man advanced and held out his hand.

"I am Tenant Mycroft Jones, the Toon Leader here," he said. "This is Stamford Rawson, our Reader, and Verner Hughes, our Toon Sarge. This is his son, Murray Hughes, the Toon Sarge of the Irregulars. But come into the Aitch-Cue House, gentlemen. We have much to talk about."

*B*y this time, the villagers had begun to emerge from the log cabins and rubble-walled houses around the plaza and the old church. Some of them, mostly young men, were carrying rifles, but the majority of them were unarmed. About half of them were women, in short deerskin or homespun dresses; there were a number of children, the younger ones almost completely naked.

"Sarge," the old man told one of the youths, "post a guard over this flying machine; don't let anybody meddle with it. And have all the noncoms and techs report here, on the double." He turned and shouted up at the truncated steeple: "Atherton, sound 'All Clear!'"

A horn, up in the belfry, began blowing, to advise the people who had run from the fields into the woods that there was no danger.

They went through the open doorway of the old stone church, and entered the big room inside. The building had evidently been gutted by fire, two centuries before, and portions of the wall had been restored. Now there was a rough plank floor, and a plank ceiling at about twelve feet; the room was apparently used as a community center. There were a number of benches and chairs, all very neatly made, and along one wall, out of the way, ten or fifteen long tables had been stacked, the tops in a pile and the trestles on them. The walls were decorated with trophies of weapons — a number of old M-12 rifles and M-16 submachine guns, all in good clean condition, a light machine rifle, two bazookas. Among them were stone and metal-tipped spears and crude hatchets and knives and clubs, the work of the wild men of the woods. A stairway led to the second floor, and it was up this that the man who bore the title of Toon Leader conducted them, to a small room furnished with a long table, a number of chairs, and several big wooden chests bound with iron.

"Sit down, gentlemen," the Toon Leader invited, going to a cupboard and producing a large bottle stopped with a corncob and a number of small cups. "It's a little early in the day," he said, "but this is a very special occasion. You smoke a pipe, I take it?" he asked Altamont. "Then try some of this; of our own growth and curing." He extended a doeskin moccasin, which seemed to be the tobacco-container.

Altamont looked at the thing dubiously, then filled his pipe from it. The oldster drew his pistol, pushed a little wooden plug into the vent, added some tow to the priming, and, aiming at the wall, snapped it. Evidently, at times the formality of plugging the vent had been over-looked; there were a number of holes in the wall there. This time, however, the pistol didn't go off. He shook out the smoldering tow, blew it into flame, and lit a candle from it, offering the light to Altamont. Loudons got out a cigar and lit it from the candle; the others filled and lighted pipes. The Toon Leader reprimed his pistol, then holstered it, took off his belt and laid it aside, an example the others followed.

They drank ceremoniously, and then seated themselves at the table. As they did, two more men came into the room; they were introduced as Alexander Barrett, the gunsmith, and Stanley Markovitch, the distill-er.

"You come, then, from the west?" the Toon Leader began by asking.

"Are you from Utah?" the gunsmith interrupted, suspiciously.

"Why, no; we're from Arizona. A place called Fort Ridgeway," Loudons said.

The others nodded, in the manner of people who wish to conceal ignorance; it was obvious that none of them had ever heard of Fort Ridgeway, or Arizona either.

"We've been in what used to be Utah," Altamont said. "There's nobody there but a few Indians, and a few whites who are even less civilized."

"You say you come from a fort? Then the wars aren't over, yet?" Sarge Hughes asked.

"The wars have been over for a long time. You know how terrible they were. You know how few in all the country were left alive," Loudons said.

"None that we know of, beside ourselves and the Scowrers until you came," the Toon Leader said.

"We have found only a few small groups, in the whole country, who have managed to save anything of the Old Times. Most of them lived in little villages and cultivated land. A few had horses, or cows. None, that we have ever found before, made guns and powder for themselves. But they remembered that they were men, and did not eat one another. Whenever we find a group of people like this, we try to persuade them to let us help them."

"Why?" the Toon Leader asked. "Why do you do this for people you've never met before? What do you want from them — from us — in return for your help?" He was speaking to Altamont, rather than to Loudons; it seemed obvious that he believed Altamont to be the leader and Loudons the subordinate.

"*B*ecause we're trying to bring back the best things of the Old Times," Altamont told him. "Look; you've had troubles, here. So have we, many times. Years when the crops failed; years of storms, or floods; troubles with these beast-men in the woods. And you were alone, as we were, with no one to help. We want to put all men who are still men in touch with one another, so that they can help each other in trouble, and work together. If this isn't done soon, everything which makes men different from beasts will soon be no more."

"He's right. One of us, alone, is helpless," the Reader said. "It is only in the Toon that there is strength. He wants to organize a Toon of all Toons."

"That's about it. We are beginning to make helicopters like the one Loudons and I came here in. We'll furnish your community with one or more of them. We can give you a radio, so that you can communicate with other communities. We can give you rifles and machine guns and ammunition, to fight the . . . the Scowrers, did you call them? And we can give you atomic engines, so that you can build machines for yourselves."

"Some of our people — Alex Barrett, here, the gunsmith, and Stan Markovitch, the distiller, and Harrison Grant, the ironworker — get their living by making things. How'd they make out, after your machines came in here?" Verner Hughes asked.

"We've thought of that; we had that problem with other groups we've helped," Loudons said. "In some communities, everybody owns everything in common; we don't have much of a problem, there. Is that the way you do it, here?"

"Well, no. If a man makes a thing, or digs it out of the ruins, or catches it in the woods, it's his."

"Then we'll work out some way. Give the machines to the people who are already in a trade, or something like that. We'll have to talk it over with you and with the people who'd be concerned."

"How is it you took so long finding us," Alex Barrett asked. "It's been two hundred or so years since the Wars."

"Alex! You see but you do not observe!" The Toon Leader rebuked. "These people have their flying machines, which are highly complicated mechanisms. They would have to make tools and machines to make them, and tools and machines to make those tools and machines. They would have to find materials, often going far in search of them. The marvel is not that they took so long, but that they did it so quickly."

"That's right," Altamont said. "Originally, Fort Ridgeway was a military research and development center. As the country became disorganized, the Government set this project up, to develop ways of improvising power and transportation and communication methods and extracting raw materials. If they'd had a little more time, they might have saved the country. As it was, they were able to keep themselves alive and keep something like civilization going at the Fort, while the whole country was breaking apart around them. Then, when the rockets stopped falling, they started to rebuild. Fortunately, more than half the technicians at the Fort were women; there was no question of them dying out. But it's only been in the last twenty years that we've been able to make nuclear-electric engines, and this is the first time any of us have gotten east of the Mississippi."

"How did your group manage to survive?" Loudons said. "You call it the Toon; I suppose that's what the word platoon has become, with time. You were, originally, a military platoon?"

"*Pla*-toon!" the white-bearded man said. "Of all the unpardonable stupidity! Of course that was what it was. And the title, Tenant, was originally *lieu*-tenant; I know that, though we have all dropped the first part of the word. That should have led me, if I'd used my wits, to deduce platoon from toon.

"Yes, sir. We were originally a platoon of soldiers, two hundred years ago, at the time when the Wars ended. The Old Toon, and the First Tenant, were guarding pows, whatever they were. The pows were all killed by a big bomb, and the First Tenant, Lieutenant Gilbert Dunbar, took his . . . his platoon and started to march to Deecee, where the Government was, but there was no Government, anymore. They fought with the people along the way. When they needed food, or ammunition, or animals to pull their wagons, they took them, and killed those who tried to prevent them. Other people joined the Toon, and when they found women whom they wanted, they took them. They did all sorts of things that would have been crimes if there had been any law, but since there was no law any longer, it was obvious that there could be no crime. The First Ten — Lieutenant — kept his men together, because he had The Books. Each evening, at the end of each day's march, he read to his men out of them.

"Finally, they came here. There had been a town here, but it had been burned and destroyed, and there were people camping in the ruins. Some of them fought and were killed; others came in and joined the platoon. At first, they built shelters around this building, and made this their fort. Then they cleared away the ruins, and built new houses. When the cartridges for the rifles began to get scarce, they began to make gunpowder, and new rifles, like these we are using now, to shoot without cartridges. Lieutenant Dunbar did this out of his own knowledge, because there is nothing in The Books about making gunpowder; the guns in The Books are rifles and shotguns and revolvers and airguns; except for the airguns, which we haven't been able to make, these all shot cartridges. As with your people, we did not die out, because we had women. Neither did we increase greatly — too many died or were killed young. But several times we've had to tear down the wall and rebuild it, to make room inside it for more houses, and we've been clearing a little more land for fields each year. We still read and follow the teachings of The Books; we have made laws for ourselves out of them."

"And we are waiting here, for the Slain and Risen One," Tenant Jones added, looking at Altamont intently. "It is impossible that He will not, sooner or later, deduce the existence of this community. If He has not done so already."

"Well, sir," the Toon Leader changed the subject abruptly, "enough of this talk about the past. If I understand rightly, it is the future in which you gentlemen are interested." He pushed back the cuff of his hunting shirt and looked at an old and worn wrist watch. "Eleven-hundred; we'll have lunch shortly. This afternoon, you will meet the other people of the Toon, and this evening, at eighteen-hundred, we'll have a mess together outdoors. Then, when we have everybody together, we can talk over your offer to help us, and decide what it is that you can give us that we can use."

"You spoke, a while ago, of what you could do for us, in return," Altamont said. "There's one thing you can do, no further away than tomorrow, if you're willing."

"And that is — ?"

"In Pittsburgh, somewhere, there is an underground crypt, full of books. Not bound and printed books; spools of microfilm. You know what that is?"

The others shook their heads. Altamont continued:

"They are spools on which strips are wound, on which pictures have been taken of books, page by page. We can make other, larger pictures from them, big enough to be read —"

"Oh, photographs, which you enlarge. I understand that. You mean, you can make many copies of them?"

"That's right. And you shall have copies, as soon as we can take the originals back to Fort Ridgeway, where we have equipment for enlarging them. But while we have information which will help us to find the crypt where the books are, we will need help in getting it open."

"Of course! This is wonderful. Copies of The Books!" the Reader exclaimed. "We thought we had the only one left in the world!"

"Not just The Books, Stamford; other books," the Toon Leader told him. "The books which are mentioned in The Books. But of course we will help you. You have a map to show where they are?"

"Not a map; just some information. But we can work out the location of the crypt."

"A ritual," Stamford Rawson said happily. "Of course."

*T*hey lunched together at the house of Toon Sarge Hughes with the Toon Leader and the Reader and five or six of the leaders of the community. The food was plentiful, but Altamont found himself wishing that the first book they found in the Carnegie Library crypt would be a cook book.

In the afternoon, he and Loudons separated. The latter attached himself to the Tenant, the Reader, and an old woman, Irene Klein, who was almost a hundred years old and was the repository and arbiter of most of the community's oral legends. Altamont, on the other hand, started, with Alex Barrett, the gunsmith, and Mordecai Ricci, the miller, to inspect the gunshop and grist mill. Joined by half a dozen more of the village craftsmen, they visited the forge and foundry, the sawmill, the wagon shop. Altamont looked at the flume, a rough structure of logs lined with sheet aluminum, and at the nitriary, a shed-roofed pit in which potassium nitrate was extracted from the community's animal refuse. Then, loading his guides into the helicopter, they took off for a visit to the powder mill on the island and a trip up the river.

They were a badly scared lot, for the first few minutes, as they watched the ground receding under them through the transparent plastic nose. Then, when nothing disastrous seemed to be happening, exhilaration took the place of fear, and by the time they set down on the tip of the island, the eight men were confirmed aviation enthusiasts. The trip up-river was an even bigger success; the high point came when Altamont set his controls for *Hover*, pointed out a snarl of driftwood in the stream, and allowed his passengers to fire one of the machine guns at it. The lead balls of their own black-powder rifles would have plunked into the waterlogged wood without visible effect; the copper-jacketed machine-gun bullets ripped it to splinters. They returned for a final visit to the distillery awed by what they had seen.

"Monty, I don't know what the devil to make of this crowd," Loudons said, that evening, after the feast, when they had entered the helicopter and prepared to retire. "We've run into some weird communities — that lot down in Old Mexico who live in the church and claim they have a divine mission to redeem the world by prayer, fasting and flagellation, or those yogis in Los Angeles —"

"Or the Blackout Boys in Detroit," Altamont added.

"That's understandable," Loudons said, "after what their ancestors went through in the Last War. But this crowd, here! The descendants of an old United States Army infantry platoon, with a fully developed religion centered on a slain and resurrected god — Normally, it would take thousands of years for a slain-god religion to develop, and then only from the field-fertility magic of primitive agriculturists. Well, you saw these people's fields from the air. Some of the members of that old platoon were men who knew the latest methods of scientific farming; they didn't need naïve fairy tales about the planting and germination of seed."

"Sure this religion isn't just a variant of Christianity?"

"Absolutely not. In the first place, these Sacred Books can't be the Bible — you heard Tenant Jones say that they mentioned firearms that used cartridges. That means that they can't be older than 1860 at the very earliest. And in the second place, this slain god wasn't crucified or put to death by any form of execution; he perished, together with his enemy, in combat, and both god and devil were later resurrected. The Enemy is supposed to be the mastermind back of these cannibal savages in the woods and also in the ruins."

"Did you get a look at these Sacred Books, or find out what they might be?"

Loudons shook his head disgustedly. "Every time I brought up the question, they evaded. The Tenant sent the Reader out to bring in this old lady, Irene Klein — she was a perfect gold mine of information about the history and traditions of the Toon, by the way — and then he sent him out on some other errand, undoubtedly to pass the word not to talk to us about their religion."

"I don't get that," Altamont said. "They showed me everything they had — their gunshop, their powder mill, their defenses, everything." He smoked in silence for a moment. "Say, this slain god couldn't be the original platoon commander, could he?"

"No. They have the greatest respect for his memory — decorate his grave regularly, drink toasts to him — but he hasn't been deified. They got the idea for this deity of theirs out of the Sacred Books." Loudons gnawed the end of his cigar and frowned. "Monty, this has me worried like the devil, because I believe that they suspect that you are the Slain and Risen One."

"Could be, at that. I know the Tenant came up to me, very respectfully, and said, 'I hope you don't think, sir, that I was presumptuous in trying to display my humble deductive abilities to *you*.'"

"What did you say?" Loudons demanded rather sharply.

"Told him certainly not; that he'd used a good quick method of demonstrating that he and his people weren't like those mindless subhumans in the woods."

"That was all right. I don't know how we're going to handle this. They only suspect that you are their deity. As it stands, now, we're on trial, here. And I get the impression that logic, not faith, seems to be their supreme religious virtue; that skepticism is a religious obligation instead of a sin. That's something else that's practically unheard of. I wish I knew —"

*T*enant Mycroft Jones, and Reader Stamford Rawson and Toon Sarge Verner Hughes, and his son Murray Hughes, sat around the bare-topped table in the room, on the second floor of the Aitch-Cue House. A lighted candle flickered in the cool breeze that came in through the open window throwing their shadows back and forth on the walls.

"Pass the tantalus, Murray," the Tenant said, and the youngest of the four handed the corncob-corked bottle to the eldest. Tenant Jones filled his cup, and then sat staring at it, while Verner Hughes thrust his pipe into the toe of the moccasin and filled it. Finally, he drank about half of the clear wild-plum brandy.

"Gentlemen, I am baffled," he confessed. "We have three alternate possibilities here, and we dare not disregard any of them. Either this man who calls himself Altamont is truly He, or he is merely what we are asked to believe, one of a community like ours, with more of the old knowledge than we possess."

"You know my views," Verner Hughes said. "I cannot believe that He was more than a man, as we are. A great, a good, a wise man, but a man and mortal."

"Let's not go into that, now." The Reader emptied his cup and took the bottle, filling it again. "You know my views, too. I hold that He is no longer upon earth in the flesh, but lives in the spirit and is only with us in the spirit. There are three possibilities, too, none of which can be eliminated. But what was your third possibility, Tenant?"

"That they are creatures of the Enemy. Perhaps that one or the other of them *is* the Enemy."

Reader Rawson, lifting his cup to his lips, almost strangled. The Hugheses, father and son, stared at Tenant Jones in horror.

"The Enemy — with such weapons and resources!" Murray Hughes gasped. Then he emptied his cup and refilled it. "No! I can't believe that; he'd have struck before this and wiped us all out!"

"Not necessarily, Murray," the Tenant replied. "Until he became convinced that his agents, the Scowrers, could do nothing against us, he would bide his time. He sits motionless, like a spider, at the center of the web; he does little himself; his agents are numerous. Or, perhaps, he wishes to recruit us into his hellish organization."

"It is a possibility," Reader Rawson admitted. "One which we can neither accept nor reject safely. And we must learn the truth as soon as possible. If this man is really He, we must not spurn Him on mere suspicion. If he is a man, come to help us, we must accept his help; if he is speaking the truth, the people who sent him could do wonders for us, and the greatest wonder would be to make us, again, a part of a civilized community. And if he is the Enemy —"

"If it is really He," Murray said, "I think we are on trial."

"What do you mean, son? Oh, I see. Of course, I don't believe he is, but that's mere doubt, not negative certainty. But if I'm wrong, if this man is truly He, we are being tested. He has come among us incognito; if we are worthy of Him, we will penetrate His disguise."

"A very pretty problem, gentlemen," the Tenant said, smacking his lips over his brandy. "For all that it may be a deadly serious one for us. There is, of course, nothing that we can do tonight. But tomorrow, we have promised to help our visitors, whoever they may be, in searching for this crypt in the city. Murray, you were to be in charge of the detail that was to accompany them. Carry on as arranged, and say nothing of our suspicions, but advise your men to keep a sharp watch on the strangers, that they may learn all they can from them. Stamford, you and Verner and I will go along. We should, if we have any wits at all, observe something."

"*L*isten to this infernal thing!" Altamont raged. "'*Wielding a gold-plated spade handled with oak from an original rafter of the Congressional Library, at three-fifteen one afternoon last week —*' One afternoon last week!" He cursed luridly. "Why couldn't that blasted magazine say *what* afternoon? I've gone over a lot of twentieth century copies of that magazine; that expression was a regular cliché with them."

Loudons looked over his shoulder at the Photostatted magazine page.

"Well, we know it was between June thirteen and nineteen, inclusive," he said. "And there's a picture of the university president, complete with gold-plated spade, breaking ground. Call it Wednesday, the sixteenth. Over there's the tip of the shadow of the old Cathedral of Learning, about a hundred yards away. There are so many inexactitudes that one'll probably cancel out another."

"That's so, and it's also pretty futile getting angry at somebody who's been dead two hundred years, but why couldn't they say Wednesday, or Monday, or Saturday, or whatever?" He checked back in the astronomical handbook, and the Photostatted pages of the old almanac, and looked over his calculations. "All right, here's the angle of the shadow, and the compass-bearing. I had a look, yesterday, when I was taking the local citizenry on that junket. The old baseball diamond at Forbes Field is plainly visible, and I located the ruins of the Cathedral of Learning from that. Here's the above-sea-level altitude of the top of the tower. After you've landed us, go up to this altitude — use the barometric altimeter, not the radar — and hold position."

Loudons leaned forward from the desk to the contraption Altamont had rigged in the nose of the helicopter — one of the telescope-sighted hunting rifles clamped in a vise, with a compass and a spirit-level under it.

"Rifle's pointing downward at the correct angle now?" he asked. "Good. Then all I have to do is hold the helicopter steady, keep it at the right altitude, level, and pointed in the right direction, and watch through the sight while you move the flag around, and direct you by radio. Why wasn't I born quintuplets?"

"Mr. Altamont! Dr. Loudons!" a voice outside the helicopter called. "Are you ready for us, now?"

Altamont went to the open door and looked out. The old Toon Leader, the Reader, Toon Sarge Hughes, his son, and four young men in buckskins with slung rifles, were standing outside.

"I have decided," the Tenant said, "that Mr. Rawson and Sarge Hughes and I would be of more help than an equal number of younger men. We may not be as active, but we know the old ruins better, especially the paths and hiding places of the Scowrers. These four young men you probably met last evening; it will do no harm to introduce them again. Birdy Edwards; Sholto Jiminez; Jefferson Burns; Murdo Olsen."

"Very pleased, Tenant, gentlemen. I met all you young men last evening; I remember you," Altamont said. "Now, if you'll all crowd in here, I'll explain what we're going to try to do."

He showed them the old picture. "You see where the shadow of a tall building falls?" he asked. "We know the location and height of this building. Dr. Loudons will hold this helicopter at exactly the position of the top of the building, and aim through the sights of the rifle, there. One of you will have this flag in his hand, and will move it back and forth; Dr. Loudons will tell us when the flag is in the sight of the rifle."

"He'll need a good pair of lungs to do that," Verner Hughes commented.

"We'll use radio. A portable set on the ground, and the helicopter's radio set." He was met, to his surprise, with looks of incomprehension. He had not supposed that these people would have lost all memory of radio communication.

"Why, that's wonderful!" the Reader exclaimed, when he explained. "You can talk directly; how much better than just sending a telegram!"

"But, finding the crypt by the shadow; that's exactly like the —" Murray Hughes began, then stopped short. Immediately, he began talking loudly about the rifle that was to be used as a surveying transit, comparing it with the ones in the big first-floor room at the Aitch-Cue House.

*L*ocating the point on which the shadow of the old Cathedral of Learning had fallen proved easier than either Altamont or Loudons had expected. The towering building was now a tumbled mass of slagged rubble, but it was quite possible to determine its original center, and with the old data from the excellent reference library at Fort Ridgeway, its height above sea level was known. After a little jockeying, the helicopter came to a hovering stop, and the slanting barrel of the rifle in the vise pointed downward along the line of the shadow that had been cast on that afternoon in June, 1993, the cross hairs of the scope-sight centered almost exactly on the spot Altamont had estimated on the map. While he peered through the sight, Loudons brought the helicopter slanting down to land on the sheet of fused glass that had once been a grassy campus.

"Well, this is probably it," Altamont said. "We didn't have to bother fussing around with that flag, after all. That hump, over there, looks as though it had been a small building, and there's nothing corresponding to it on the city map. That may be the bunker over the stair-head to the crypt."

They began unloading equipment — a small portable nuclear-electric conversion unit, a powerful solenoid-hammer, crowbars and entrenching tools, tins of blasting-plastic. They took out the two hunting rifles, and the auto-carbines, and Altamont showed the young men of Murray Hughes' detail how to use them.

"If you'll pardon me, sir," the Tenant said to Altamont, "I think it would be a good idea if your companion went up in the flying machine and circled around over us, to keep watch for Scowrers. There are quite a few of them, particularly farther up the rivers, to the east, where the damage was not so great and they can find cellars and shelters and buildings to live in."

"Good idea; that way, we won't have to put out guards," Altamont said. "From the looks of this, we'll need everybody to help dig into that thing. Hand out one of the portable radios, Jim, and go up to about a thousand feet. If you see anything suspicious, give us a yell, and then spray it with bullets, and find out what it is afterward."

They waited until the helicopter had climbed to position and was circling above, and then turned their attention to the place where the sheet of fused earth and stone bulged upward. It must have been almost ground-zero of one of the hydrogen-bombs; the wreckage of the Cathedral of Learning had fallen predominantly to the north, and the Carnegie Library was tumbled to the east.

"I think the entrance would be on this side, toward the Library," Altamont said. "Let's try it, to begin with."

He used the solenoid-hammer, slowly pounding a hole into the glaze, and placed a small charge of the plastic explosive. Chunks of the lavalike stuff pelted down between the little mound and the huge one of the old library, blowing a hole six feet in diameter and two and a half deep, revealing concrete bonded with crushed steel-mill slag.

"We missed the door," he said. "That means we'll have to tunnel in through who knows how much concrete. Well —"

*H*e used a second and larger charge, after digging a hole a foot deep. When he and his helpers came up to look, they found a large mass of concrete blown out, and solid steel behind it. Altamont cut two more holes sidewise, one on either side of the blown-out place, and fired a charge in each of them, bringing down more concrete. He found that he hadn't missed the door, after all. It had merely been concreted over.

A few more shots cleared it, and after some work, they got it open. There was a room inside, concrete-floored and entirely empty. With the others crowding behind him, Altamont stood in the doorway and inspected the interior with his flashlight; he heard somebody back of him say something about a most peculiar sort of a dark-lantern. Across the small room, on the opposite wall, was a bronze plaque.

It carried quite a lengthy inscription, including the names of all the persons and institutions participating in the microfilm project. The History Department at the Fort would be most interested in that, but the only thing that interested Altamont was the statement that the floor had been laid over the trapdoor leading to the vaults where the microfilms were stored. He went outside to the radio.

"Hello, Jim. We're inside, but the films are stored in an underground vault, and we have to tear up a concrete floor," he said. "Go back to the village and gather up all the men you can carry, and tools. Hammers and picks and short steel bars. I don't want to use explosives inside. The interior of the crypt oughtn't to be damaged, and I don't know what a blast in here might do to the film, and I don't want to take chances."

"No, of course not. How thick do you think this floor is?"

"Haven't the least idea. Plenty thick, I'd say. Those films would have to be well buried, to shield them from radioactivity. We can expect that it'll take some time."

"All right. I'll be back as soon as I can."

The helicopter turned and went windmilling away, over what had been the Golden Triangle, down the Ohio.

Altamont went back to the little concrete bunker and sat down, lighting his pipe. Murray Hughes and his four riflemen spread out, one circling around the glazed butte that had been the Cathedral of Learning, another climbing to the top of the old library, and the others taking positions to the south and east.

Altamont sat in silence, smoking his pipe and trying to form some conception of the wealth under that concrete floor. It was no use. Jim Loudons probably understood a little more nearly what those books would mean to the world of today, and what they could do toward shaping the world of the future. There was a library at Fort Ridgeway, and it was an excellent one — for its purpose. In 1996, when the rockets had come crashing down, it had contained the cream of the world's technological knowledge — and very little else. There was a little fiction, a few books of ideas, just enough to give the survivors a tantalizing glimpse of the world of their fathers. But now —

A rifle banged to the south and east, and banged again. Either Murray Hughes or Birdy Edwards — it was one of the two hunting rifles from the helicopter. On the heels of the reports, they heard a voice shouting: "Scowrers! A lot of them, coming from up the river!" A moment later, there was a light whip-crack of one of the long muzzle-loaders, from the top of the old Carnegie Library, and Altamont could see a wisp of grey-white smoke drifting away from where it had been fired. He jumped to his feet and raced for the radio, picking it up and bringing it to the bunker.

Tenant Jones, old Reader Rawson, and Verner Hughes had caught up their rifles. The Tenant was shouting, "Come on in! Everybody, come in!" The boy on top of the library began scrambling down. Another came running from the direction of the half-demolished Cathedral of Learning, a third from the baseball field that had served as Altamont's point of reference the afternoon before. The fourth, Murray Hughes, was running in from the ruins of the old Carnegie Tech buildings, and Birdy Edwards sped up the main road from Shenley Park. Once or twice, as he ran, Murray Hughes paused, turned, and fired behind him.

Then his pursuers came into sight. They ran erect, and they wore a few rags of skin garments, and they carried spears and hatchets and clubs, so they were probably classifiable as men. Their hair was long and unkempt; their bodies were almost black with dirt and from the sun. A few of them were yelling; most of them ran silently. They ran more swiftly than the boy they were pursuing; the distance between them narrowed every moment. There were at least fifty of them.

Verner Hughes' rifle barked; one of them dropped. As coolly as though he were shooting squirrels instead of his son's pursuers, he dropped the butt of his rifle to the ground, poured a charge of powder, patched a ball and rammed it home, replaced the ramrod. Tenant Jones fired then, and then Birdy Edwards joined them and began shooting with the telescope-sighted hunting rifle. The young man who had been north of the Cathedral of Learning had one of the auto-carbines; Altamont had providently set the fire-control for semi-auto before giving it to him. He dropped to one knee and began to empty the clip, shooting slowly and deliberately, picking off the runners who were in the lead. The boy who had started to climb down off the library halted, fired his flintlock, and began reloading it. And Altamont, sitting down and propping his elbows on his knees, took both hands to the automatic which was his only weapon, emptying the magazine and replacing it. The last three of the savages he shot in the back; they had had enough and were running for their lives.

So far, everybody was safe. The boy in the library came down through a place where the wall had fallen. Murray Hughes stopped running and came slowly toward the bunker, putting a fresh clip into his rifle. The others came drifting in.

"Altamont, calling Loudons," the scientist from Fort Ridgeway was saying into the radio. "Monty to Jim; can you hear me, Jim?"

Silence.

"We'd better get ready for another attack," Birdy Edwards said. "There's another gang coming from down that way. I never saw so many Scowrers!"

"Maybe there's a reason, Birdy," Tenant Jones said. "The Enemy is after big game, this time."

"Jim! Where the devil are you?" Altamont fairly yelled into the radio, and as he did, he knew the answer. Loudons was in the village, away from the helicopter, gathering tools and workers. Nothing to do but keep on trying.

"Here they come!" Reader Rawson warned.

"How far can these rifles be depended on?" Birdy Edwards wanted to know.

Altamont straightened, saw the second band of savages approaching, about four hundred yards away.

"Start shooting now," he said. "Aim for the upper part of their bodies."

The two auto-loading rifles began to crack. After a few shots, the savages took cover. Evidently they understood the capabilities and limitations of the villagers' flintlocks; this was a terrifying surprise to them.

"Jim!" Altamont was almost praying into the radio. "Come in, Jim!"

"What is it, Monty? I was outside."

Altamont told him.

"Those fellows you had up with you yesterday; think they could be trusted to handle the guns? A couple of them are here with me," Loudons inquired.

"Take a chance on it; it won't cost you anything but my life, and that's not worth much at present."

"All right; hold on. We'll be along in a few minutes."

"Loudons is bringing the helicopter," he told the others. "All we have to do is hold on, here, till he comes."

A naked savage raised his head from behind what might, two hundred years ago, have been a cement park-bench, a hundred yards away. Reader Stamford Rawson promptly killed him and began reloading.

"I think you're right, Tenant," he said. "The Scowrers have never attacked in bands like this before. They must have had a powerful reason, and I can think of only one."

"That's what I'm beginning to think, too," Verner Hughes agreed. "At least, we have eliminated the third of your possibilities, Tenant. And I think probably the second, as well."

Altamont wondered what they were double-talking about. There wasn't any particular mystery about the mass attack of the wild men to him. Debased as they were, they still possessed speech and the ability to transmit experiences. No matter how beclouded in superstition, they still remembered that aircraft dropped bombs, and bombs killed people, and where people had been killed, they would find fresh meat. They had seen the helicopter circling about, and had heard the blasting; everyone in the area had been drawn to the scene as soon as Loudons had gone down the river.

Maybe they had forgotten that aircraft also carried guns. At least, when they sprang to their feet and started to run at the return of the helicopter, many did not run far.

*A*ltamont and Loudons shook hands many times in front of the Aitch-Cue House, and listened to many good wishes, and repeated their promise to return. Most of the microfilmed books were still stored in the old church; they were taking away with them only the catalogue and a few of the more important works. Finally, they entered the helicopter. The crowd shouted farewell, as they rose.

Altamont, at the controls, waited until they had gained five thousand feet, then turned on a compass-course for Colony Three.

"I can't wait till we're in radio-range of the Fort, to report this, Jim," he said. "Of all the wonderful luck! And I don't yet know which is more important; finding those books, or finding those people. In a few years, when we can get them supplied with modern equipment and instructed in its use —"

"I'm not very happy about it, Monty," Loudons confessed. "I keep thinking about what's going to happen to them."

"Why, nothing's going to happen to them. They're going to be given the means of producing more food, keeping more of them alive, having more leisure to develop themselves in —"

"Monty; I saw the Sacred Books."

"The deuce! What were they?"

"It. One volume; a collection of works. We have it at the Fort; I've read it. How I ever missed all the clues — You see Monty, what I'm worried about is what's going to happen to those people when they find out that we're not really Sherlock Holmes and Dr. Watson."

Temple Trouble

Through a haze of incense and altar smoke, Yat-Zar looked down from his golden throne at the end of the dusky, many-pillared temple. Yat-Zar was an idol, of gigantic size and extraordinarily good workmanship; he had three eyes, made of turquoises as big as doorknobs, and six arms. In his three right hands, from top to bottom, he held a sword with a flame-shaped blade, a jeweled object of vaguely phallic appearance, and, by the ears, a rabbit. In his left hands were a bronze torch with burnished copper flames, a big goblet, and a pair of scales with an egg in one pan balanced against a skull in the other. He had a long bifurcate beard made of gold wire, feet like a bird's, and other rather startling anatomical features. His throne was set upon a stone plinth about twenty feet high, into the front of which a doorway opened; behind him was a wooden screen, elaborately gilded and painted.

Directly in front of the idol, Ghullam the high priest knelt on a big blue and gold cushion. He wore a gold-fringed robe of dark blue, and a tall conical gold miter, and a bright blue false beard, forked like the idol's golden one: he was intoning a prayer, and holding up, in both hands, for divine inspection and approval, a long curved knife. Behind him, about thirty feel away, stood a square stone altar, around which four of the lesser priests, in light blue robes with less gold fringe and dark-blue false beards, were busy with the preliminaries to the sacrifice. At considerable distance, about halfway down the length of the temple, some two hundred worshipers — a few substantial citizens in gold-fringed tunics, artisans in tunics without gold fringe, soldiers in mail hauberks and plain steel caps, one officer in ornately gilded armor, a number of peasants in nondescript smocks, and women of all classes — were beginning to prostrate themselves on the stone floor.

Ghullam rose to his feet, bowing deeply to Yat-Zar and holding the knife extended in front of him, and backed away toward the altar. As he did, one of the lesser priests reached into a fringed and embroidered sack and pulled out a live rabbit, a big one, obviously of domestic breed, holding it by the ears while one of his fellows took it by the hind legs. A third priest caught up a silver pitcher, while the fourth fanned the altar fire with a sheet-silver fan. As they began chanting antiphonally, Ghullam turned and quickly whipped the edge of his knife across the rabbit's throat. The priest with the pitcher stepped in to catch the blood, and when the rabbit was bled, it was laid on the fire. Ghullam and his four assistants all shouted together, and the congregation shouted in response.

The high priest waited as long as was decently necessary and then, holding the knife in front of him, stepped around the prayer-cushion and went through the door under the idol into the Holy of Holies. A boy in novice's white robes met him and took the knife, carrying it reverently to a fountain for washing. Eight or ten under-priests, sitting at a long table, rose and bowed, then sat down again and resumed their eating and drinking. At another table, a half-dozen upper priests nodded to him in casual greeting.

Crossing the room, Ghullam went to the Triple Veil in front of the House of Yat-Zar, where only the highest of the priesthood might go, and parted the curtains, passing through, until he came to the great gilded door. Here he fumbled under his robe and produced a small object like a mechanical pencil, inserting the pointed end in a tiny hole in the door and pressing on the other end. The door opened, then swung shut behind him, and as it locked itself, the lights came on within. Ghullam removed his miter and his false beard, tossing them aside on a table, then undid his sash and peeled out of his robe. His regalia discarded, he stood for a moment in loose trousers and a soft white shirt, with a pistollike weapon in a shoulder holster under his left arm — no longer Ghullam the high priest of Yat-Zar, but now Stranor Sleth, resident agent on this time-line of the Fourth Level Proto-Aryan Sector for the Transtemporal Mining Corporation. Then he opened a door at the other side of the anteroom and went to the antigrav shaft, stepping over the edge and floating downward.

*T*here were temples of Yat-Zar on every time-line of the Proto-Aryan Sector, for the worship of Yat-Zar was ancient among the Hulgun people of that area of paratime, but there were only a few which had such installations as this, and all of them were owned and operated by Transtemporal Mining, which had the fissionable ores franchise for this sector. During the ten elapsed centuries since Transtemporal had begun operations on this sector, the process had become standardized. A few

First Level paratimers would transpose to a selected time-line and abduct an upper-priest of Yat-Zar, preferably the high priest of the temple at Yoldav or Zurb. He would be drugged and transposed to the First Level, where he would receive hypnotic indoctrination and, while unconscious, have an operation performed on his ears which would enable him to hear sounds well above the normal audible range. He would be able to hear the shrill sonar-cries of bats, for instance, and, more important, he would be able to hear voices when the speaker used a First Level audio-frequency step-up phone. He would also receive a memory-obliteration from the moment of his abduction, and a set of pseudo-memories of a visit to the Heaven of Yat-Zar, on the other side of the sky. Then he would be returned to his own time-line and left on a mountain top far from his temple, where an unknown peasant, leading a donkey, would always find him, return him to the temple, and then vanish inexplicably.

Then the priest would begin hearing voices, usually while serving at the altar. They would warn of future events, which would always come to pass exactly as foretold. Or they might bring tidings of things happening at a distance, the news of which would not arrive by normal means for days or even weeks. Before long, the holy man who had been carried alive to the Heaven of Yat-Zar would acquire a most awesome reputation as a prophet, and would speedily rise to the very top of the priestly hierarchy.

Then he would receive two commandments from Yat-Zar. The first would ordain that all lower priests must travel about from temple to temple, never staying longer than a year at any one place. This would insure a steady influx of newcomers personally unknown to the local upper-priests, and many of them would be First Level paratimers. Then, there would be a second commandment: A house must be built for Yat-Zar, against the rear wall of each temple. Its dimensions were minutely stipulated; its walls were to be of stone, without windows, and there was to be a single door, opening into the Holy of Holies, and before the walls were finished, the door was to be barred from within. A triple veil of brocaded fabric was to be hung in front of this door. Sometimes such innovations met with opposition from the more conservative members of the hierarchy: when they did, the principal objector would be seized with a sudden and violent illness; he would recover if and when he withdrew his objections.

Very shortly after the House of Yat-Zar would be completed, strange noises would be heard from behind the thick walls. Then, after a while, one of the younger priests would announce that he had been commanded in a vision to go behind the veil and knock upon the door.

Going behind the curtains, he would use his door-activator to let himself in, and return by paratime-conveyer to the First Level to enjoy a well-earned vacation. When the high priest would follow him behind the veil, after a few hours, and find that he had vanished, it would be announced as a miracle. A week later, an even greater miracle would be announced. The young priest would return from behind the Triple Veil, clad in such raiment as no man had ever seen, and bearing in his hands a strange box. He would announce that Yat-Zar had commanded him to build a new temple in the mountains, at a place to be made known by the voice of the god speaking out of the box.

This time, there would be no doubts and no objections. A procession would set out, headed by the new revelator bearing the box, and when the clicking voice of the god spoke rapidly out of it, the site would be marked and work would begin. No local labor would ever be employed on such temples; the masons and woodworkers would be strangers, come from afar and speaking a strange tongue, and when the temple was completed, they would never be seen to leave it. Men would say that they had been put to death by the priest and buried under the altar to preserve the secrets of the god. And there would always be an idol to preserve the secrets of the god. And there would always be an idol of Yat-Zar, obviously of heavenly origin, since its workmanship was beyond the powers of any local craftsman. The priests of such a temple would be exempt, by divine decree, from the rule of yearly travel.

Nobody, of course, would have the least idea that there was a uranium mine in operation under it, shipping ore to another time-line. The Hulgun people knew nothing about uranium, and neither did they as much as dream that there were other time-lines. The secret of paratime transposition belonged exclusively to the First Level civilization which had discovered it, and it was a secret that was guarded well.

*S*tranor Sleth, dropping to the bottom of the antigrav shaft, cast a hasty and instinctive glance to the right, where the freight conveyers were. One was gone, taking its cargo over hundreds of thousands of para-years to the First Level. Another had just returned, empty, and a third was receiving its cargo from the robot mining machines far back under the mountain. Two young men and a girl, in First Level costumes, sat at a bank of instruments and visor-screens, handling the whole operation, and six or seven armed guards, having inspected the newly-arrived conveyer and finding that it had picked up nothing inimical en route, were relaxing and lighting cigarettes. Three of them, Stranor Sleth noticed, wore the green uniforms of the Paratime Police.

"When did those fellows get in?" he asked the people at the control desk, nodding toward the green-clad newcomers.

"About ten minutes ago, on the passenger conveyer," the girl told him. "The Big Boy's here. Brannad Klav. And a Paratime Police officer. They're in your office."

"Uh huh; I was expecting that," Stranor Sleth nodded. Then he turned down the corridor to the left.

Two men were waiting for him, in his office. One was short and stocky, with an angry, impatient face — Brannad Klav, Transtemporal's vice president in charge of operations. The other was tall and slender with handsome and entirely expressionless features; he wore a Paratime Police officer's uniform, with the blue badge of hereditary nobility on his breast, and carried a sigma-ray needler in a belt holster.

"Were you waiting long, gentlemen?" Stranor Sleth asked. "I was holding Sunset Sacrifice up in the temple."

"No, we just got here," Brannad Klav said. "This is Verkan Vall, Mavrad of Nerros, special assistant to Chief Tortha of the Paratime Police, Stranor Sleth, our resident agent here."

Stranor Sleth touched hands with Verkan Vall.

"I've heard a lot about you, sir," he said. "Everybody working in paratime has, of course. I'm sorry we have a situation here that calls for your presence, but since we have, I'm glad you're here in person. You know what our trouble is, I suppose?"

"In a general way," Verkan Vall replied. "Chief Tortha, and Brannad Klav, have given me the main outline, but I'd like to have you fill in the details."

"Well, I told you everything," Brannad Klav interrupted impatiently. "It's just that Stranor's let this blasted local king, Kurchuk, get out of control. If I —" He stopped short, catching sight of the shoulder holster under Stranor Sleth's left arm. "Were you wearing that needler up in the temple?" he demanded.

"You're blasted right I was!" Stranor Sleth retorted. "And anytime I can't arm myself for my own protection on this time-line, you can have my resignation. I'm not getting into the same jam as those people at Zurb."

"Well, never mind about that," Verkan Vall intervened. "Of course Stranor Sleth has a right to arm himself; I wouldn't think of being caught without a weapon on this time-line, myself. Now, Stranor, suppose you tell me what's been happening, here, from the beginning of this trouble."

"It started, really, about five years ago, when Kurchuk, the King of Zurb, married this Chuldun princess, Darith, from the country over beyond the Black Sea, and made her his queen, over the heads of about a dozen daughters of the local nobility, whom he'd married previously. Then he brought in this Chuldun scribe, Labdurg, and made him Overseer of the Kingdom — roughly, prime minister. There was a lot of dissatisfaction about that, and for a while it looked as though he was going to have a revolution on his hands, but he brought in about five thousand Chuldun mercenaries, all archers — these Hulguns can't shoot a bow worth beans — so the dissatisfaction died down, and so did most of the leaders of the disaffected group. The story I get is that this Labdurg arranged the marriage, in the first place. It looks to me as though the Chuldun emperor is intending to take over the Hulgun kingdoms, starting with Zurb.

"Well, these Chulduns all worship a god called Muz-Azin. Muz-Azin is a crocodile with wings like a bat and a lot of knife blades in his tail. He makes this Yat-Zar look downright beautiful. So do his habits. Muz-Azin fancies human sacrifices. The victims are strung up by the ankles on a triangular frame and lashed to death with iron-barbed whips. Nasty sort of a deity, but this is a nasty time-line. The people here get a big kick out of watching these sacrifices. Much better show than our bunny-killing. The victims are usually criminals, or overage or incorrigible slaves, or prisoners of war.

"Of course, when the Chulduns began infiltrating the palace, they brought in their crocodile-god, too, and a flock of priests, and King Kurchuk let them set up a temple in the palace. Naturally, we preached against this heathen idolatry in our temples, but religious bigotry isn't one of the numerous imperfections of this sector. Everybody's deity is as good as anybody else's — indifferentism, I believe, is the theological term. Anyhow, on that basis things went along fairly well, till two years ago, when we had this run of bad luck."

"Bad luck!" Brannad Klav snorted. "That's the standing excuse of every incompetent!"

"Go on, Stranor; what sort of bad luck?" Verkan Vall asked.

"Well, first we had a drought, beginning in early summer, that burned up most of the grain crop. Then, when that broke, we got heavy rains and hailstorms and floods, and that destroyed what got through the dry spell. When they harvested what little was left, it was obvious there'd be a famine, so we brought in a lot of grain by conveyer and distributed it from the temples — miraculous gift of Yat-Zar, of course. Then the main office on First Level got scared about flooding this time-line with a lot of unaccountable grain and were afraid we'd make the people suspicious, and ordered it stopped.

"Then Kurchuk, and I might add that the kingdom of Zurb was the hardest hit by the famine, ordered his army mobilized and started an invasion of the Jumdun country, south of the Carpathians, to get grain. He got his army chopped up, and only about a quarter of them got back, with no grain. You ask me, I'd say that Labdurg framed it to happen that way. He advised Kurchuk to invade, in the first place, and I mentioned my suspicion that Chombrog, the Chuldun Emperor, is planning to move in on the Hulgun kingdoms. Well, what would be smarter than to get Kurchuk's army smashed in advance?"

"How did the defeat occur?" Verkan Vall asked. "Any suspicion of treachery?"

"Nothing you could put your finger on, except that the Jumduns seemed to have pretty good intelligence about Kurchuk's invasion route and battle plans. It could have been nothing worse than stupid tactics on Kurchuk's part. See, these Hulguns, and particularly the Zurb Hulguns, are spearmen. They fight in a fairly thin line, with heavy-armed infantry in front and light infantry with throwing-spears behind. The nobles fight in light chariots, usually at the center of the line, and that's where they were at this Battle of Jorm. Kurchuk himself was at the center, with his Chuldun archers massed around him.

"The Jumduns use a lot of cavalry, with long swords and lances, and a lot of big chariots with two javelin men and a driver. Well, instead of ramming into Kurchuk's center, where he had his archers, they hit the extreme left and folded it up, and then swung around behind and hit the right from the rear. All the Chuldun archers did was stand fast around the king and shoot anybody who came close to them: they were left pretty much alone. But the Hulgun spearmen were cut to pieces. The battle ended with Kurchuk and his nobles and his archers making a fighting retreat, while the Jumdun cavalry were chasing the spearmen every which way and cutting them down or lancing them as they ran.

"Well, whether it was Labdurg's treachery or Kurchuk's stupidity, in either case, it was natural for the archers to come off easiest and the Hulgun spearmen to pay the butcher's bill. But try and tell these knuckle-heads anything like that! Muz-Azin protected the Chulduns, and Yat-Zar let the Hulguns down, and that was all there was to it. The Zurb temple started losing worshipers, particularly the families of the men who didn't make it back from Jorm.

"If that had been all there'd been to it, though, it still wouldn't have hurt the mining operations, and we could have got by. But what really tore it was when the rabbits started to die." Stranor Sleth picked up a cigar from his desk and bit the end, spitting it out disgustedly. "Tula-remia, of course," he said, touching his lighter to the tip. "When that hit, they started going over to Muz-Azin in droves, not only at Zurb but all over the Six Kingdoms. You ought to have seen the house we had for Sunset Sacrifice, this evening! About two hundred, and we used to get two thousand. It used to be all two men could do to lift the offering box at the door, afterward, and all the money we took in tonight I could put in one pocket!" The high priest used language that would have been considered unclerical even among the Hulguns.

Verkan Vall nodded. Even without the quickie hypno-mech he had taken for this sector, he knew that the rabbit was domesticated among the Proto-Aryan Hulguns and was their chief meat animal. Hulgun rabbits were even a minor import on the First Level, and could be had at all the better restaurants in cities like Dhergabar. He mentioned that.

"That's not the worst of it," Stranor Sleth told him. "See, the rabbit's sacred to Yat-Zar. Not taboo; just sacred. They have to use a specially consecrated knife to kill them — consecrating rabbit knives has always been an item of temple revenue — and they must say a special prayer before eating them. We could have got around the rest of it, even the Battle of Jorm — punishment by Yat-Zar for the sin of apostasy — but Yat-Zar just wouldn't make rabbits sick. Yat-Zar thinks too well of rabbits to do that, and it'd not been any use claiming he would. So there you are."

"Well, I take the attitude that this situation is the result of your incompetence," Brannad Klav began, in a bullyragging tone. "You're not only the high priest of this temple, you're the acknowledged head of the religion in all the Hulgun kingdoms. You should have had more hold on the people than to allow anything like this to happen."

"Hold on the people!" Stranor Sleth fairly howled, appealing to Verkan Vall. "What does he think a religion is, on this sector, anyhow? You think these savages dreamed up that six-armed monstrosity, up there, to express their yearning for higher things, or to symbolize their moral ethos, or as a philosophical escape-hatch from the dilemma of causation? They never even heard of such matters. On this sector, gods are strictly utilitarian. As long as they take care of their worshipers, they get their sacrifices: when they can't put out, they have to get out. How do you suppose these Chulduns, living in the Caucasus Mountains, got the idea of a god like a crocodile, anyhow? Why, they got it from Homran traders, people from down in the Nile Valley. They had a god, once, something basically like a billy goat, but he let them get licked in a couple of battles, so out he went. Why, all the deities on this sector have hyphenated names, because they're combinations of several deities, worshiped in one person. Do you know anything about the history of this sector?" he asked the Paratime Police officer.

"Well, it develops from an alternate probability of what we call the Nilo-Mesopotamian Basic sector-group," Verkan Vall said. "On most Nilo-Mesopotamian sectors, like the Macedonian Empire Sector, or the Alexandrian-Roman or Alexandrian-Punic or Indo-Turanian or Europo-American, there was an Aryan invasion of Eastern Europe and Asia Minor about four thousand elapsed years ago. On this sector, the ancestors of the Aryans came in about fifteen centuries earlier, as neolithic savages, about the time that the Sumerian and Egyptian civilizations were first developing, and overran all southeast Europe, Asia Minor and the Nile Valley. They developed to the bronze-age culture of the civilizations they overthrew, and then, more slowly, to an iron-age culture. About two thousand years ago, they were using hardened steel and building large stone cities, just as they do now. At that time, they reached cultural stasis. But as for their religious beliefs, you've described them quite accurately. A god is only worshiped as long as the people think him powerful enough to aid and protect them; when they lose that confidence, he is discarded and the god of some neighboring people is adopted instead." He turned to Brannad Klav. "Didn't Stranor report this situation to you when it first developed?" he asked. "I know he did; he speaks of receiving shipments of grain by conveyer for temple distribution. Then why didn't you report it to Paratime Police? That's what we have a Paratime Police Force for."

"Well, yes, of course, but I had enough confidence in Stranor Sleth to think that he could handle the situation himself. I didn't know he'd gone slack —"

"Look, I can't make weather, even if my parishioners think I can," Stranor Sleth defended himself. "And I can't make a great military genius out of a blockhead like Kurchuk. And I can't immunize all the rabbits on this time-line against tularemia, even if I'd had any reason to expect a tularemia epidemic, which I hadn't because the disease is unknown on this sector; this is the only outbreak of it anybody's ever heard of on any Proto-Aryan time-line."

"No, but I'll tell you what you could have done," Verkan Vall told him. "When this Kurchuk started to apostatize, you could have gone to him at the head of a procession of priests, all paratimers and all armed with energy-weapons, and pointed out his spiritual duty to him, and if he gave you any back talk, you could have pulled out that needler and rayed him down and then cried, 'Behold the vengeance of Yat-Zar upon the wicked king!' I'll bet any sum at any odds that his successor would have thought twice about going over to Muz-Azin, and none of these other kings would have even thought once about it."

"Ha, that's what I wanted to do!" Stranor Sleth exclaimed. "And who stopped me? I'll give you just one guess."

"Well, it seems there was slackness here, but it wasn't Stranor Sleth who was slack," Verkan Vall commented.

"Well! I must say; I never thought I'd hear an officer of the Paratime Police criticizing me for trying to operate inside the Paratime Transposition Code!" Brannad Klav exclaimed.

Verkan Vall, sitting on the edge of Stranor Sleth's desk, aimed his cigarette at Brannad Klav like a blaster.

"Now, look," he began. "There is one, and only one, inflexible law regarding outtime activities. The secret of paratime transposition must be kept inviolate, and any activity tending to endanger it is prohibited. That's why we don't allow the transposition of any object of extraterrestrial origin to any time-line on which space travel has not been developed. Such an object may be preserved, and then, after the local population begin exploring the planet from whence it came, there will be dangerous speculations and theories as to how it arrived on Terra at such an early date. I came within inches, literally, of getting myself killed, not long ago, cleaning up the result of a violation of that regulation. For the same reason, we don't allow the export, to outtime natives, of manufactured goods too far in advance of their local culture. That's why, for instance, you people have to hand-finish all those big Yat-Zar idols, to remove traces of machine work. One of those things may be around, a few thousand years from now, when these people develop a mechanical civilization. But as far as raying down this Kur-chuk is concerned, these Hulguns are completely nonscientific. They wouldn't have the least idea what happened. They'd believe that Yat-Zar struck him dead, as gods on this plane of culture are supposed to do, and if any of them noticed the needler at all, they'd think it was just a holy amulet of some kind."

"But the law is the law —" Brannad Klav began.

Verkan Vall shook his head. "Brannad, as I understand, you were promoted to your present position on the retirement of Salvan Marth, about ten years ago; up to that time, you were in your company's financial department. You were accustomed to working subject to the First Level Commercial Regulation Code. Now, any law binding upon our people at home, on the First Level, is inflexible. It has to be. We found out, over fifty centuries ago, that laws have to be rigid and without discretionary powers in administration in order that people may be able to predict their effect and plan their activities accordingly. Naturally, you became conditioned to operating in such a climate of legal inflexibility.

"But in paratime, the situation is entirely different. There exist, within the range of the Ghaldron-Hesthor paratemporal-field generator, a number of time-lines of the order of ten to the hundred-thousandth power. In effect, that many different worlds. In the past ten thousand years, we have visited only the tiniest fraction of these, but we have found everything from time-lines inhabited only by subhuman ape-men to Second Level civilizations which are our own equal in every respect but knowledge of paratemporal transposition. We even know of one Second Level civilization which is approaching the discovery of an interstellar hyperspatial drive, something we've never even come close to. And in between are every degree of savagery, barbarism and civilization. Now, it's just not possible to frame any single code of laws applicable to conditions on all of these. The best we can do is prohibit certain flagrantly immoral types of activity, such as slave-trading, introduction of new types of narcotic drugs, or out-and-out piracy and brigandage. If you're in doubt as to the legality of anything you want to do outtime, go to the Judicial Section of the Paratime Commission and get an opinion on it. That's where you made your whole mistake. You didn't find out just how far it was allowable for you to go."

He turned to Stranor Sleth again. "Well, that's the background, then. Now tell me about what happened yesterday at Zurb."

"Well, a week ago, Kurchuk came out with this decree closing our temple at Zurb and ordering his subjects to perform worship and make money offerings to Muz-Azin. The Zurb temple isn't a mask for a mine: Zurb's too far south for the uranium deposits. It's just a center for propaganda and that sort of thing. But they have a House of Yat-Zar, and a conveyer, and most of the upper-priests are paratimers. Well, our man there, Tammand Drav, alias Khoram, defied the king's order, so Kurchuk sent a company of Chuldun archers to close the temple and arrest the priests. Tammand Drav got all his people who were in the temple at the time into the House of Yat-Zar and transposed them back to the First Level. He had orders" — Stranor Sleth looked meaningly at Brannad Klav — "not to resist with energy-weapons or even ultrasonic paralyzers. And while we're on the subject of letting the local yokels see too much, about fifteen of the under-priests he took to the First Level were Hulgun natives."

"Nothing wrong about that: they'll get memory-obliteration and pseudo-memory treatment," Verkan Vall said. "But he should have been allowed to needle about a dozen of those Chulduns. Teach the beggars to respect Yat-Zar in the future. Now, how about the six priests who were outside the temple at the time? All but one were paratimers. We'll have to find out about them, and get them out of Zurb."

"That'll take some doing," Stranor Sleth said. "And it'll have to be done before sunset tomorrow. They are all in the dungeon of the palace citadel, and Kurchuk is going to give them to the priests of Muz-Azin to be sacrificed tomorrow evening."

"How'd you learn that?" Verkan Vall asked.

"Oh, we have a man in Zurb, not connected with the temple," Stranor Sleth said. "Name's Crannar Jurth; calls himself Kranjur, locally. He has a swordmaker's shop, employs about a dozen native journeymen and apprentices who hammer out the common blades he sells in the open market. Then, he imports a few high-class alloy-steel blades from the First Level, that'll cut through this local low-carbon armor like cheese. Fits them with locally-made hilts and sells them at unbelievable prices to the nobility. He's Swordsmith to the King; picks up all the inside palace dope. Of course, he was among the first to accept the New Gospel and go over to Muz-Azin. He has a secret room under his shop, with his conveyer and a radio.

"What happened was this: These six priests were at a consecration ceremony at a rabbit-ranch outside the city, and they didn't know about the raid on the temple. On their way back, they were surrounded by Chuldun archers and taken prisoner. They had no weapons but their sacrificial knives." He threw another dirty look at Brannad Klav. "So they're due to go up on the triangles at sunset tomorrow."

"We'll have to get them out before then," Verkan Vall stated. "They're our people, and we can't let them down; even the native is under our protection, whether he knows it or not. And in the second place, if those priests are sacrificed to Muz-Azin," he told Brannad Klav, "you can shut down everything on this time-line, pull out or disintegrate your installations, and fill in your mine-tunnels. Yat-Zar will be through on this time-line, and you'll be through along with him. And considering that your fissionables franchise for this sector comes up for renewal next year, your company will be through in this paratime area."

"You believe that would happen?" Brannad Klav asked anxiously.

"I know it will, because I'll put through a recommendation to that effect, if those six men are tortured to death tomorrow," Verkan Vall replied. "And in the fifty years that I've been in the Police Department, I've only heard of five such recommendations being ignored by the commission. You know, Fourth Level Mineral Products Syndicate is after your franchise. Ordinarily, they wouldn't have a chance of getting it, but with this, maybe they will, even without my recommendation.

This was all your fault, for ignoring Stranor Sleth's proposal and for denying those men the right to carry energy weapons."

"Well, we were only trying to stay inside the Paratime Code," Brannad Klav pleaded. "If it isn't too late, now, you can count on me for every cooperation." He fiddled with some papers on the desk. "What do you want me to do to help?"

"I'll tell you that in a minute." Verkan Vall walked to the wall and looked at the map, then returned to Stranor Sleth's desk. "How about these dungeons?" he asked. "How are they located, and how can we get in to them?"

"I'm afraid we can't," Stranor Sleth told him. "Not without fighting our way in. They're under the palace citadel, a hundred feet below ground. They're spatially co-existent with the heavy water barriers around one of our company's plutonium piles on the First Level, and below surface on any unoccupied time-line I know of, so we can't transpose in to them. This palace is really a walled city inside a city. Here, I'll show you."

Going around the desk, he sat down and, after looking in the index-screen, punched a combination on the keyboard. A picture, projected from the microfilm-bank, appeared on the view-screen. It was an air-view of the city of Zurb — taken, the high priest explained, by infrared light from an airboat over the city at night. It showed a city of an entirely pre-mechanical civilization, with narrow streets, lined on either side by low one and two story buildings. Although there would be considerable snow in winter, the roofs were usually flat, probably massive stone slabs supported by pillars within. Even in the poorer sections, this was true except for the very meanest houses and out-buildings, which were thatched. Here and there, some huge pile of masonry would rear itself above its lower neighbors, and, where the streets were wider, occasional groups of large buildings would be surrounded by battlemented walls. Stranor Sleth indicated one of the larger of these.

"Here's the palace," he said. "And here's the temple of Yat-Zar, about half a mile away." He touched a large building, occupying an entire block; between it and the palace was a block-wide park, with lawns and trees on either side of a wide roadway connecting the two.

"Now, here's a detailed view of the palace." He punched another combination; the view of the City was replaced by one, taken from directly overhead, of the walled palace area. "Here's the main gate, in front, at the end of the road from the temple," he pointed out. "Over here, on the left, are the slaves' quarters and the stables and workshops and store houses and so on. Over here, on the other side, are the nobles' quarters. And this," — he indicated a towering structure at the rear of the walled enclosure — "is the citadel and the royal dwelling. Audience hall on this side; harem over here on this side. A wide stone platform, about fifteen feet high, runs completely across the front of the citadel, from the audience hall to the harem. Since this picture was taken, the new temple of Muz-Azin was built right about here." He indicated that it extended out from the audience hall into the central courtyard. "And out here on the platform, they've put up about a dozen of these triangles, about twelve feet high, on which the sacrificial victims are whipped to death."

"Yes. About the only way we could get down to the dungeons would be to make an airdrop onto the citadel roof and fight our way down with needlers and blasters, and I'm not willing to do that as long as there's any other way," Verkan Vall said. "We'd lose men, even with needlers against bows, and there's a chance that some of our equipment might be lost in the mêlée and fall into outtime hands. You say this sacrifice comes off tomorrow at sunset?"

"That would be about actual sunset plus or minus an hour; these people aren't astronomers, they don't even have good sundials, and it might be a cloudy day," Stranor Sleth said. "There will be a big idol of Muz-Azin on a cart, set about here." He pointed. "After the sacrifice, it is to be dragged down this road, outside, to the temple of Yat-Zar, and set up there. The temple is now occupied by about twenty Chuldun mercenaries and five or six priests of Muz-Azin. They haven't, of course, got into the House of Yat-Zar; the door's of impervium steel, about six inches thick, with a plating of collapsed nickel under the gilding. It would take a couple of hours to cut through it with our best atomic torch; there isn't a tool on this time-line that could even scratch it. And the insides of the walls are lined with the same thing."

"Do you think our people have been tortured, yet?" Verkan Vall asked.

"No." Stranor Sleth was positive. "They'll be fairly well treated, until the sacrifice. The idea's to make them last as long as possible on the triangles; Muz-Azin likes to see a slow killing, and so does the mob of spectators."

"That's good. Now, here's my plan. We won't try to rescue them from the dungeons. Instead, we'll transpose back to the Zurb temple from the First Level, in considerable force — say a hundred or so men — and march on the palace, to force their release. You're in constant radio communication with all the other temples on this time-line, I suppose?"

"Yes, certainly."

"All right. Pass this out to everybody, authority Paratime Police, in my name, acting for Tortha Karf. I want all paratimers who can possibly be spared to transpose to First Level immediately and rendezvous at the

First Level terminal of the Zurb temple conveyer as soon as possible. Close down all mining operations, and turn over temple routine to the native under-priests. You can tell them that the upper-priests are retiring to their respective Houses of Yat-Zar to pray for the deliverance of the priests in the hands of King Kurchuk. And everybody is to bring back his priestly regalia to the First Level; that will be needed." He turned to Brannad Klav. "I suppose you keep spare regalia in stock on the First Level?"

"Yes, of course; we keep plenty of everything in stock. Robes, miters, false beards of different shades, everything."

"And these big Yat-Zar idols: they're mass-produced on the First Level? You have one available now? Good. I'll want some alterations made on one. For one thing, I'll want it plated heavily, all over, with collapsed nickel. For another, I'll want it fitted with antigrav units and some sort of propulsion-units, and a loud-speaker, and remote control.

"And, Stranor, you get in touch with this swordmaker, Crannar Jurth, and alert him to co-operate with us. Tell him to start calling Zurb temple on his radio about noon tomorrow, and keep it up till he gets an answer. Or, better, tell him to run his conveyer to his First Level terminal, and bring with him an extra suit of clothes appropriate to the role of journeyman-mechanic. I'll want to talk to him, and furnish him with special equipment. Got all that? Well, carry on with it, and bring your own paratimers, priests and mining operators, back with you as soon as you've taken care of everything. Brannad, you come with me, now. We're returning to First Level immediately. We have a lot of work to do, so let's get started."

"Anything I can do to help, just call on me for it," Brannad Klav promised earnestly. "And, Stranor, I want to apologize. I'll admit, now, that I ought to have followed your recommendations, when this situation first developed."

By noon of the next day, Verkan Vall had at least a hundred men gathered in the big room at the First Level fissionables refinery at Jarnabar, spatially co-existent with the Fourth Level temple of Yat-Zar at Zurb. He was having a little trouble distinguishing between them, for every man wore the fringed blue robe and golden miter of an upper-priest, and had his face masked behind a blue false beard. It was, he admitted to himself, a most ludicrous-looking assemblage; one of the most ludicrous things about it was the fact that it would have inspired only pious awe in a Hulgun of the Fourth Level Proto-Aryan Sector.

About half of them were priests from the Transtemporal Mining Corporation's temples; the other half were members of the Paratime Police. All of them wore, in addition to their temple knives, holstered sigma-ray needlers. Most of them carried ultrasonic paralyzers, eighteen-inch batonlike things with bulbous ends. Most of the Paratime Police and a few of the priests also carried either heat-ray pistols or neutron-disruption blasters; Verkan Vall wore one of the latter in a left-hand belt holster.

The Paratime Police were lined up separately for inspection, and Stranor Sleth, Tammand Drav of the Zurb temple, and several other high priests were checking the authenticity of their disguises. A little apart from the others, a Paratime Policeman, in high priest's robes and beard, had a square box slung in front of him; he was fiddling with knobs and buttons on it, practicing. A big idol of Yat-Zar, on antigravity, was floating slowly about the room in obedience to its remote controls, rising and lowering, turning about and pirouetting gracefully.

"Hey, Vall!" he called to his superior. "How's this?"

The idol rose about five feet, turned slowly in a half-circle, moved to the right a little, and then settled slowly toward the floor.

"Fine, fine, Horv," Verkan Vall told him, "but don't set it down on anything, or turn off the antigravity. There's enough collapsed nickel-plating on that thing to sink it a yard in soft ground."

"I don't know what the idea of that was," Brannad Klav, standing beside him, said. "Understand, I'm not criticizing. I haven't any right to, under the circumstances. But it seems to me that armoring that thing in collapsed nickel was an unnecessary precaution."

"Maybe it was," Verkan Vall agreed. "I sincerely hope so. But we can't take any chances. This operation has to be absolutely right. Ready, Tammand? All right; first detail into the conveyer."

He turned and strode toward a big dome of fine metallic mesh, thirty feet high and sixty in diameter, at the other end of the room. Tammand Drav, and his ten paratimer priests, and Brannad Klav, and ten Paratime Police, followed him in. One of the latter slid shut the door and locked it; Verkan Vall went to the control desk, at the center of the dome, and picked up a two-foot globe of the same fine metallic mesh, opening it and making some adjustments inside, then attaching an electric cord and closing it. He laid the globe on the floor near the desk and picked up the hand battery at the other end of the attached cord.

"Not taking any chances at all, are you?" Brannad Klav asked, watching this operation with interest.

"I never do, unnecessarily. There are too many necessary chances that have to be taken, in this work." Verkan Vall pressed the button on the hand battery. The globe on the floor flashed and vanished. "Yesterday, five paratimers were arrested. Any or all of them could have had door-activators with them. Stranor Sleth says they were not tortured, but that is a purely inferential statement. They may have been, and the use of the activator may have been extorted from one of them. So I want a look at the inside of that conveyer-chamber before we transpose into it."

He laid the hand battery, with the loose-dangling wire that had been left behind, on the desk, then lit a cigarette. The others gathered around, smoking and watching, careful to avoid the place from which the globe had vanished. Thirty minutes passed, and then, in a queer iridescence, the globe reappeared. Verkan Vall counted ten seconds and picked it up, taking it to the desk and opening it to remove a small square box. This he slid into a space under the desk and flipped a switch. Instantly, a view-screen lit up and a three-dimensional picture appeared — the interior of a big room a hundred feet square and some seventy in height. There was a big desk and a radio; tables, couches, chairs and an arms-rack full of weapons, and at one end, a remarkably clean sixty-foot circle on the concrete floor, outlined in faintly luminous red.

"How about it?" Verkan Vall asked Tammand Drav. "Anything wrong?"

The Zurb high priest shook his head. "Just as we left it," he said. "Nobody's been inside since we left."

One of the policemen took Verkan Vall's place at the control desk and threw the master switch, after checking the instruments. Immediately, the paratemporal-transposition field went on with a humming sound that mounted to a high scream, then settled to a steady drone. The mesh dome flickered with a cold iridescence and vanished, and they were looking into the interior of a great fissionables refinery plant, operated by paratimers on another First Level time-line. The structural details altered, from time-line to time-line, as they watched. Buildings appeared and vanished. Once, for a few seconds, they were inside a cool, insulated bubble in the midst of molten lead. Tammand Drav jerked a thumb at it, before it vanished.

"That always bothers me," he said. "Bad place for the field to go weak. I'm fussy as an old hen about inspection of the conveyer, on account of that."

"Don't blame you," Verkan Vall agreed. "Probably the cooling system of a breeder-pile."

They passed more swiftly, now, across the Second Level and the Third. Once they were in the midst of a huge land battle, with great tanklike vehicles spouting flame at one another. Another moment was spent in an air bombardment. On any time-line, this section of East Europe was a natural battleground. Once a great procession marched toward them, carrying red banners and huge pictures of a coarse-faced man with a black mustache — Verkan Vall recognized the environment as Fourth Level Europo-American Sector. Finally, as the transposition-rate slowed, they saw a clutter of miserable thatched huts, in the rear of a granite wall of a Fourth Level Hulgun temple of Yat-Zar — a temple not yet infiltrated by Transtemporal Mining Corporation agents. Finally, they were at their destination. The dome around them became visible, and an overhead green light flashed slowly on and off.

Verkan Vall opened the door and stepped outside, his needler drawn. The House of Yat-Zar was just as he had seen it in the picture photographed by the automatic reconnaissance-conveyer. The others crowded outside after him. One of the regular priests pulled off his miter and beard and went to the radio, putting on a headset. Verkan Vall and Tammand Drav snapped on the visiscreen, getting a view of the Holy of Holies outside.

There were six men there, seated at the upper-priests' banquet table, drinking from golden goblets. Five of them wore the black robes with green facings which marked them as priests of Muz-Azin; the sixth was an officer of the Chuldun archers, in gilded mail and helmet.

"Why, those are the sacred vessels of the temple!" Tammand Drav cried, scandalized. Then he laughed in self-ridicule. "I'm beginning to take this stuff seriously, myself; time I put in for a long vacation. I was actually shocked at the sacrilege!"

"Well, let's overtake the infidels in their sins," Verkan Vall said. "Paralyzers will be good enough."

He picked up one of the bulb-headed weapons, and unlocked the door. Tammand Drav and another of the priests of the Zurb temple following and the others crowding behind, they passed out through the veils, and burst into the Holy of Holies. Verkan Vall pointed the bulb of his paralyzer at the six seated men and pressed the button; other paralyzers came into action, and the whole sextet were knocked senseless. The officer rolled from his chair and fell to the floor in a clatter of armor. Two of the priests slumped forward on the table. The others merely sank back in their chairs, dropping their goblets.

"Give each one of them another dose, to make sure," Verkan Vall directed a couple of his own men. "Now, Tammand; any other way into the main temple beside that door?"

"Up those steps," Tammand Drav pointed. "There's a gallery along the side; we can cover the whole room from there."

"Take your men and go up there. I'll take a few through the door. There'll be about twenty archers out there, and we don't want any of them loosing any arrows before we can knock them out. Three minutes be time enough?"

"Easily. Make it two," Tammand Drav said.

*H*e took his priests up the stairway and vanished into the gallery of the temple. Verkan Vall waited until one minute had passed and then, followed by Brannad Klav and a couple of Paratime Policemen, he went under the plinth and peered out into the temple. Five or six archers, in steel caps and sleeveless leather jackets sewn with steel rings, were gathered around the altar, cooking something in a pot on the fire. Most of the others, like veteran soldiers, were sprawled on the floor, trying to catch a short nap, except half a dozen, who crouched in a circle, playing some game with dice — another almost universal military practice.

The two minutes were up. He aimed his paralyzer at the men around the altar and squeezed the button, swinging it from one to another and knocking them down with a bludgeon of inaudible sound. At the same time, Tammand Drav and his detail were stunning the gamblers. Stepping forward and to one side, Verkan Vall, Brannad Klav and the others took care of the sleepers on the floor. In less than thirty seconds, every Chuldun in the temple was incapacitated.

"All right, make sure none of them come out of it prematurely," Verkan Vall directed. "Get their weapons, and be sure nobody has a knife or anything hidden on him. Who has the syringe and the sleep-drug ampoules?"

Somebody had, it developed, who was still on the First Level, to come up with the second conveyer load. Verkan Vall swore. Something like this always happened, on any operation involving more than half a dozen men.

"Well, some of you stay here: patrol around, and use your paralyzers on anybody who even twitches a muscle." Ultrasonics were nice, effective, humane police weapons, but they were unreliable. The same dose that would keep one man out for an hour would paralyze another for no more than ten or fifteen minutes. "And be sure none of them are playing 'possum."

He went back through the door under the plinth, glancing up at the decorated wooden screen and wondering how much work it would take to move the new Yat-Zar in from the conveyers. The five priests and the archer-captain were still unconscious; one of the policemen was searching them.

"Here's the sort of weapons these priests carry," he said, holding up a short iron mace with a spiked head. "Carry them on their belts." He tossed it on the table, and began searching another knocked-out hierophant. "Like this — *Hey!* Look at this, will you!"

He drew his hand from under the left side of the senseless man's robe and held up a sigma-ray needler. Verkan Vall looked at it and nodded grimly.

"Had it in a regular shoulder holster," the policeman said, handing the weapon across the table. "What do you think?"

"Find anything else funny on him?"

"Wait a minute." The policeman pulled open the robe and began stripping the priest of Muz-Azin; Verkan Vall came around the table to help. There was nothing else of a suspicious nature.

"Could have got it from one of the prisoners, but I don't like the familiar way he's wearing that holster," Verkan Vall said. "Has the conveyer gone back, yet?" When the policeman nodded, he continued: "When it returns, take him to the First Level. I hope they bring up the sleep-drug with the next load. When you get him back, take him to Dhergabar by strato-rocket immediately, and make sure he gets back alive. I want him questioned under narco-hypnosis by a regular Paratime Commission psycho-technician, in the presence of Chief Tortha Karf and some responsible Commission official. This is going to be hot stuff."

Within an hour, the whole force was assembled in the temple. The wooden screen had presented no problem — it slid easily to one side — and the big idol floated on antigravity in the middle of the temple. Verkan Vall was looking anxiously at his watch.

"It's about two hours to sunset," he said, to Stranor Sleth. "But as you pointed out, these Hulguns aren't astronomers, and it's a bit cloudy. I wish Crannar Jurth would call in with something definite."

Another twenty minutes passed. Then the man at the radio came out into the temple.

"O. K.!" he called. "The man at Crannar Jurth's called in. Crannar Jurth contacted him with a midget radio he has up his sleeve; he's in the palace courtyard now. They haven't brought out the victims, yet, but Kurchuk has just been carried out on his throne to that platform in front of the citadel. Big crowd gathering in the inner courtyard; more in the streets outside. Palace gates are wide open."

"That's it!" Verkan Vall cried. "Form up; the parade's starting. Brannad, you and Tammand and Stranor and I in front; about ten men with paralyzers a little behind us. Then Yat-Zar, about ten feet off the ground, and then the others. Forward — *ho-o!*"

*T*hey emerged from the temple and started down the broad roadway toward the palace. There was not much of a crowd, at first. Most of Zurb had flocked to the palace earlier; the lucky ones in the courtyard and the late comers outside. Those whom they did meet stared at them in open-mouthed amazement, and then some, remembering their doubts and blasphemies, began howling for forgiveness. Others — a substantial majority — realizing that it would be upon King Kurchuk that the real weight of Yat-Zar's six hands would fall, took to their heels, trying to put as much distance as possible between them and the palace before the blow fell.

As the procession approached the palace gates, the crowds were thicker, made up of those who had been unable to squeeze themselves inside. The panic was worse, here, too. A good many were trampled and hurt in the rush to escape, and it became necessary to use paralyzers to clear a way. That made it worse: everybody was sure that Yat-Zar was striking sinners dead left and right.

Fortunately, the gates were high enough to let the god through without losing altitude appreciably. Inside, the mob surged back, clearing a way across the courtyard. It was only necessary to paralyze a few here, and the levitated idol and its priestly attendants advanced toward the stone platform, where the king sat on his throne, flanked by court functionaries and black-robed priests of Muz-Azin. In front of this, a rank of Chuldun archers had been drawn up.

"Horv; move Yat-Zar forward about a hundred feet and up about fifty," Verkan Vall directed. "Quickly!"

As the six-armed anthropomorphic idol rose and moved closer toward its saurian rival, Verkan Vall drew his needler, scanning the assemblage around the throne anxiously.

"Where is the wicked King?" a voice thundered — the voice of Stranor Sleth, speaking into a midget radio tuned to the loud-speaker inside the idol. *"Where is the blasphemer and desecrator, Kurchuk?"*

"There's Labdurg, in the red tunic, beside the throne," Tammand Drav whispered. "And that's Ghromdur, the Muz-Azin high priest, beside him."

Verkan Vall nodded, keeping his eyes on the group on the platform. Ghromdur, the high priest of Muz-Azin, was edging backward and reaching under his robe. At the same time, an officer shouted an order, and the Chuldun archers drew arrows from their quivers and fitted them to their bowstrings. Immediately, the ultrasonic paralyzers of the advancing paratimers went into action, and the mercenaries began dropping.

"Lay down your weapons, fools!" the amplified voice boomed at them. "Lay down your weapons or you shall surely die! Who are you, miserable wretches, to draw bows against Me?"

At first a few, then all of them, the Chulduns lowered or dropped their weapons and began edging away to the sides. At the center, in front of the throne, most of them had been knocked out. Verkan Vall was still watching the Muz-Azin high priest intently; as Ghromdur raised his arm, there was a flash and a puff of smoke from the front of Yat-Zar — the paint over the collapsed nickel was burned off, but otherwise the idol was undamaged. Verkan Vall swung up his needler and rayed Ghromdur dead; as the man in the green-faced black robes fell, a blaster clattered on the stone platform.

"Is that your puny best, Muz-Azin?" the booming voice demanded. *"Where is your high priest now?"*

"Horv; face Yat-Zar toward Muz-Azin," Verkan Vall said over his shoulder, drawing his blaster with his left hand. Like all First Level people, he was ambidextrous, although, like all paratimers, he habitually concealed the fact while outtime. As the levitated idol swung slowly to look down upon its enemy on the built-up cart, Verkan Vall aimed the blaster and squeezed.

In a spot less than a millimeter in diameter on the crocodile idol's side, a certain number of neutrons in the atomic structure of the stone from which it was carved broke apart, becoming, in effect, atoms of hydrogen. With a flash and a bang, the idol burst and vanished. Yat-Zar gave a dirty laugh and turned his back on the cart, which was now burning fiercely facing King Kurchuk again.

"Get your hands up, all of you!" Verkan Vall shouted, in the First Level language, swinging the stubby muzzle of the blaster and the knob-tipped twin tubes of the needler to cover the group around the throne, "Come forward, before I start blasting!"

Labdurg raised his hands and stepped forward. So did two of the priests of Yat-Zar. They were quickly seized by Paratime Policemen who swarmed up onto the platform and disarmed. All three were carrying sigma-ray needlers, and Labdurg had a blaster as well.

King Kurchuk was clinging to the arms of his throne, a badly frightened monarch trying desperately not to show it. He was a big man, heavy-shouldered, black-bearded; under ordinary circumstances he would probably have cut an imposing figure, in his gold-washed mail and his golden crown. Now his face was a dirty grey, and he was biting nervously at his lower lip. The others on the platform were in even worse state. The Hulgun nobles were grouped together, trying to disassociate themselves from both the king and the priests of Muz-Azin. The latter were staring in a daze at the blazing cart from which their idol had just been blasted. And the dozen men who were to have done the actual work of the torture-sacrifice had all dropped their whips and were fairly gibbering in fear.

Yat-Zar, manipulated by the robed paratimer, had taken a position directly above the throne and was lowering slowly. Kurchuk stared up at the massive idol descending toward him, his knuckles white as he clung to the arms of his throne. He managed to hold out until he could feel the weight of the idol pressing on his head. Then, with a scream, he hurled himself from the throne and rolled forward almost to the edge of the platform. Yat-Zar moved to one side, swung slightly and knocked the throne toppling, and then settled down on the platform. To Kurchuk, who was rising cautiously on his hands and knees, the big idol seemed to be looking at him in contempt.

"*Where are my holy priests, Kurchuk?*" Stranor Sleth demanded in to his sleeve-hidden radio. "*Let them be brought before me, alive and unharmed, or it shall be better for you had you never been born!*"

The six priests of Yat-Zar, it seemed, were already being brought onto the platform by one of Kurchuk's nobles. This noble, whose name was Yorzuk, knew a miracle when he saw one, and believed in being on the side of the god with the heaviest artillery. As soon as he had seen Yat-Zar coming through the gate without visible means of support, he had hastened to the dungeons with half a dozen of his personal retainers and ordered the release of the six captives. He was now escorting them onto the platform, assuring them that he had always been a faithful servant of Yat-Zar and had been deeply grieved at his sovereign's apostasy.

"*Hear my word, Kurchuk,*" Stranor Sleth continued through the loud-speaker in the idol. "*You have sinned most vilely against me, and were I a cruel god, your fate would be such as no man has ever before suffered. But I am a merciful god; behold, you may gain forgiveness in my sight. For thirty days, you shall neither eat meat nor drink wine, nor shall you wear gold nor fine raiment, and each day shall you go to my temple and beseech me for my forgiveness. And on the thirty-first day, you shall set out, barefoot and clad in the garb of a slave, and journey to my temple that is in the mountains over above Yoldav, and there will I forgive you, after you have made sacrifice to me. I, Yat-Zar, have spoken!"*

The king started to rise, babbling thanks.

"Rise not before me until I have forgiven you!" Yat-Zar thundered. *"Creep out of my sight upon your belly, wretch!"*

The procession back to the temple was made quietly and sedately along an empty roadway. Yat-Zar seemed to be in a kindly humor; the people of Zurb had no intention of giving him any reason to change his mood. The priests of Muz-Azin and their torturers had been flung into the dungeon. Yorzuk, appointed regent for the duration of Kur-chuk's penance, had taken control and was employing Hulgun spearmen and hastily-converted Chuldun archers to restore order and, inciden-tally, purge a few of his personal enemies and political rivals. The priests, with the three prisoners who had been found carrying First Level weapons among them and Yat-Zar floating triumphantly in front, entered the temple. A few of the devout, who sought admission after them, were told that elaborate and secret rites were being held to cleanse the profaned altar, and sent away.

Verkan Vall and Brannad Klav and Stranor Sleth were in the conveyer chamber, with the Paratime Policemen and the extra priests; along with them were the three prisoners. Verkan Vall pulled off his false beard and turned to face these. He could see that they all recognized him.

"Now," he began, "you people are in a bad jam. You've violated the Paratime Transposition Code, the Commercial Regulation Code, and the First Level Criminal Code, all together. If you know what's good for you, you'll start talking."

"I'm not saying anything till I have legal advice," the man who had been using the local alias of Labdurg replied. "And if you're through searching me, I'd like to have my cigarettes and lighter back."

"Smoke one of mine, for a change," Verkan Vall told him. "I don't know what's in yours beside tobacco." He offered his case and held a light for the prisoner before lighting his own cigarette. "I'm going to be sure you get back to the First Level alive."

The former Overseer of the Kingdom of Zurb shrugged. "I'm still not talking," he said.

"Well, we can get it all out of you by narco-hypnosis, anyhow," Verkan Vall told him. "Besides, we got that man of yours who was here at the temple when we came in. He's being given a full treatment, as a presumed outtime native found in possession of First Level weapons. If you talk now it'll go easier with you."

The prisoner dropped the cigarette on the floor and tramped it out.

"Anything you cops get out of me, you'll have to get the hard way," he said. "I have friends on the First Level who'll take care of me."

"I doubt that. They'll have their hands full taking care of themselves, after this gets out." Verkan Vall turned to the two in the black robes. "Either of you want to say anything?" When they shook their heads, he nodded to a group of his policemen; they were hustled into the conveyer. "Take them to the First Level terminal and hold them till I come in. I'll be along with the next conveyer load."

*T*he conveyer flashed and vanished. Brannad Klav stared for a moment at the circle of concrete floor from whence it had disappeared. Then he turned to Verkan Vall.

"I still can't believe it," he said. "Why, those fellows were First Level paratimers. So was that priest, Ghromdur: the one you rayed."

"Yes, of course. They worked for your rivals, the Fourth Level Mineral Products Syndicate; the outfit that was trying to get your Proto-Aryan Sector fissionables franchise away from you. They operate on this sector already; have the petroleum franchise for the Chuldun country, east of the Caspian Sea. They export to some of these internal-combustion-engine sectors, like Europo-American. You know, most of the wars they've been fighting, lately, on the Europo-American Sector have been, at least in part, motivated by rivalry for oil fields. But now that the Europo-Americans have begun to release nuclear energy, fissionables have become more important than oil. In less than a century, it's predicted that atomic energy will replace all other forms of power. Mineral Products Syndicate wanted to get a good source of supply for uranium, and your Proto-Aryan Sector franchise was worth grabbing.

"I had considered something like this as a possibility when Stranor, here, mentioned that tularemia was normally unknown in Eurasia on this sector. That epidemic must have been started by imported germs. And I knew that Mineral Products has agents at the court of the Chuldun emperor, Chombrog: they have to, to protect their oil wells on his eastern frontiers. I spent most of last night checking up on some stuff by video-transcription from the Paratime Commission's microfilm library at Dhergabar. I found out, for one thing, that while there is a King Kurchuk of Zurb on every time-line for a hundred para-years on either side of this one, this is the only time-line on which he married a

Princess Darith of Chuldun, and it's the only time-line on which there is any trace of a Chuldun scribe named Labdurg.

"That's why I went to all the trouble of having that Yat-Zar plated with collapsed nickel. If there were disguised paratimers among the Muz-Azin party at Kurchuk's court, I expected one of them to try to blast our idol when we brought it into the palace. I was watching Ghromdur and Labdurg in particular; as soon as Ghromdur used his blaster, I needled him. After that, it was easy."

"Was that why you insisted on sending that automatic viewer on ahead?"

"Yes. There was a chance that they might have planted a bomb in the House of Yat-Zar, here. I knew they'd either do that or let the place entirely alone. I suppose they were so confident of getting away with this that they didn't want to damage the conveyer or the conveyer chamber. They expected to use them, themselves, after they took over your company's franchise."

"Well, what's going to be done about it by the Commission?" Brannad Klav wanted to know.

"Plenty. The syndicate will probably lose their paratime license; any of its officials who had guilty knowledge of this will be dealt with according to law. You know, this was a pretty nasty business."

"You're telling me!" Stranor Sleth exclaimed. "Did you get a look at those whips they were going to use on our people? Pointed iron barbs a quarter-inch long braided into them, all over the lash-ends!"

"Yes. Any punitive action you're thinking about taking on these priests of Muz-Azin — the natives, I mean — will be ignored on the First Level. And that reminds me: you'd better work out a line of policy, pretty soon."

"Well, as for the priests and the torturers, I think I'll tell Yorzuk to have them sold to the Bhunguns, to the east. They're always in the market for galley slaves," Stranor Sleth said. He turned to Brannad Klav. "And I'll want six gold crowns made up, as soon as possible. Strictly Hulgun design, with Yat-Zar religious symbolism, very rich and ornate, all slightly different. When I give Kurchuk absolution, I'll crown him at the altar in the name of Yat-Zar. Then I'll invite in the other five Hulgun kings, lecture them on their religious duties, make them confess their secret doubts, forgive them, and crown them, too. From then on, they can all style themselves as ruling by the will of Yat-Zar."

"And from then on, you'll have all of them eating out of your hand," Verkan Vall concluded. "You know, this will probably go down in Hulgun history as the Reformation of Ghullam the Holy. I've always wondered whether the theory of the divine right of kings was invented by the kings, to establish their authority over the people, or by the priests, to establish *their* authority over the kings. It works about as well one way as the other."

"What I can't understand is this," Brannad Klav said. "It was entirely because of my respect for the Paratime Code that I kept Stranor Sleth from using Fourth Level weapons and other techniques to control these people with a show of apparent miraculous powers. But this Fourth Level Mineral Products Syndicate was operating in violation of the Paratime Code by invading our franchise area. Why didn't they fake up a supernatural reign of terror to intimidate these natives?"

"Ha, exactly because they *were* operating illegally," Verkan Vall replied. "Suppose they had started using needlers and blasters and antigravity and nuclear-energy around here. The natives would have thought it was the power of Muz-Azin, of course, but what would you have thought? You'd have known, as soon as they tried it, that First Level paratimers were working against you, and you'd have laid the facts before the Commission, and this time-line would have been flooded with Paratime Police. They had to conceal their operations not only from the natives, as you do, but also from us. So they didn't dare make public use of First Level techniques.

"Of course, when we came marching into the palace with that idol on antigravity, they knew, at once, what was happening. I have an idea that they only tried to blast that idol to create a diversion which would permit them to escape — if they could have got out of the palace, they'd have made their way, in disguise, to the nearest Mineral Products Syndicate conveyer and transposed out of here. I realized that they could best delay us by blasting our idol, and that's why I had it plated with collapsed nickel. I think that where they made their mistake was in allowing Kurchuk to have those priests arrested, and insisting on sacrificing them to Muz-Azin. If it hadn't been for that, the Paratime Police wouldn't have been brought into this, at all.

"Well, Stranor, you'll want to get back to your temple, and Brannad and I want to get back to the First Level. I'm supposed to take my wife to a banquet in Dhergabar, tonight, and with the fastest strato-rocket, I'll just barely make it."

www.ingramcontent.com/pod-product-compliance
Lightning Source LLC
Chambersburg PA
CBHW050803250626
47155CB00005B/2194